# Red Cape Publishing Presents...

# The A-Z of Horror: O is for Outbreak

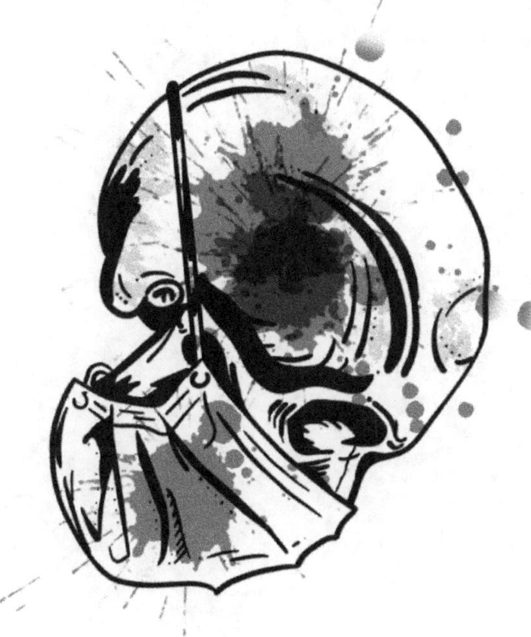

With special thanks to


Lesley Drane

Craig Crawford

Blazing Minds

**Support us at**
www.patreon.com/redcapepublishing
www.ko-fi.com/redcape

# Contents

## You Have Been Cleared for Entry

### Damir Salkovic

They were supposed to get off from the ship at nine, but it was well past ten now and the gangway was still up, the disembarkation crew nowhere in sight. From her position by the promenade doors, Emily could see the empty concrete docks, the murky sea sloshing at the waterline, the rectangular blocks of the terminal building. A strip of blue, cloudless Florida sky peered down, cut up by the gangways leading to Deck Four. Dark shapes prowled it busily, like sharks: helicopters, the sound of their blades kept out by the heavy glass.

Emily shivered in the airconditioned chill, rubbed her shoulders. Suddenly she missed the solicitous attention of the ever-present crew, the captain's comforting voice over the speakers. It felt strange, being up here in the Odysseus First Class Lounge, muzak piping down from the speakers, watching the empty port below. It made her feel like she was the last person in the world, like in the silly TV shows John enjoyed watching. Civilization breaking down overnight, cars piled up on silent highways, the undead shambling down previously bustling streets. Somehow the lounge felt like the safer option, even packed as it was with grumbling, overfed holidaymakers in a hurry to leave. She could hold onto the memory of their seven days on the seas, a different sun-soaked port almost every day, pretending she was in her twenties again, footloose and without a care in the world. Every hour spent on the ship meant a reprieve from dreary reality, one featureless day blending into the next, a relentless trickling away of time.

If they were delayed longer, they'd miss their flight home. *At least they could put out an announcement,* she thought, *or hand out complimentary drinks*. She glanced over at John, who was reclining in one of the booths, his phone mere inches from the tip of his nose.

A pang went through her that had nothing to do with the cold in the room.

Joanie wasn't picking up. They had taken turns calling her since the ship had pulled into port late last night, received nothing but her voicemail. Seven days of complete isolation had sounded great to begin with: no social media posts or calls, not so much as a text message. But now their daughter was halfway across a continent and a viral pandemic, some sort of superflu, was ravaging the nation. Emily had overheard snippets from other travelers on the cruise, and had caught part of a news bulletin in Spanish in a beach bar in Costa Rica. She couldn't understand the language, but the accompanying graphic spoke clearly enough. San Diego, where Joanie lived, had been placed under curfew; red circles, indicating the spread of the disease, bloomed over cities along both coasts.

Emily sat down across from her husband, struggling to control her thoughts. Tried to convince herself that Joanie would be fine. Five months ago they had tried to persuade their daughter to come and stay with them, at least until she got back on her feet. But Joanie wouldn't hear of it. She had always been resilient, refused to be daunted. Emily had no idea which side of the family *those* traits had come from, but she was grateful for them, proud of their headstrong daughter.

Until now, when all she wanted was her little girl next to her. Safe from harm.

She watched John put the phone away, the blank expression on his face failing to hide his anxiety. He said nothing, avoided her eyes.

"It's in all the big cities now."

Without wanting to, Emily turned toward the speaker. He and his companion seemed to have stepped right out of an eighties cable sitcom: both beefy and sunburned, clad in garish, neon-bright outfits, the woman's hair an impossibly bleached blonde. White-stockinged feet in sandals. A red cap advertising some deep-sea-fishing outfit sat askew on the man's peeling bald head. "That's plain as day. Big cities, and all those inner-city projects they got there."

He chuckled and glanced around the lounge, as if trying to engage the passengers in conversation. When no one took up the bait, he continued, undaunted. "Big city folks, they try to tell the rest of us how to live our lives. Let's see how well they handle their own business."

Emily did her best to ignore him, but a black dread loomed at the back of her mind, threatening to overwhelm her. Joanie was fine. Bugs came and went every season; the only special thing about this one was a slightly higher mortality rate. Small children and the elderly were more vulnerable, and Joanie fell into neither category. Joanie was probably busy, or out with friends. Getting hold of her was hard enough under normal circumstances.

"She's not picking up." John sounded exasperated, like he was expecting her to take care of the situation. "I left her another voicemail. That's four, or five, at least."

"She'll be fine," Emily said. Beyond the other set of doors, the ones leading back into the ship, a handful of crew members and a man in a blue tunic -- a ship's officer, she assumed -- had huddled together and were discussing something, their postures carefully guarded. Every now and then, one of them would look at the passengers in the lounge with a vague expression of concern. Emily tried to focus on their faces, to discern what they were saying, but the lounge was full of murmurs, the glass opaque with reflections.

*Stop overreacting. You do this to yourself all the time. Everything's fine.*

To take her mind off her unease, she studied the other passengers in Group Orange. They were going to great lengths to ignore those from other cabins, poking their smartphones or muttering into them, regurgitating variations on what they'd already been told, or read on their news apps: the ship was in port, there was some kind of delay, so-and-so would need to pick them up from the airport. Some appeared oblivious of the crisis unfolding around them, yammering about their cruise, the excursions they'd gone on. A lean, competent-looking young woman was bouncing a crying baby on her hip, smiling and talking at the screen of the phone she held at arms' length. For a moment, Emily allowed herself to be lulled by the woman's easy confidence. Then she thought of the baby, which prompted another thought of Joanie. She turned her own phone in slick hands, fighting an urge to call again.

Speakers chimed and the captain's voice came on, calm and cultured, informing the passengers that their debarkation would take a little longer, thanking them for their patience. Paperwork had to be cleared with the port authorities: there had been some sort of misunderstanding about the new sanitation protocols. A groan of disbelief went up from the gathering. Arms were thrown up, complaints vented at the ceiling. Emily felt a numb despair creep over her. She glanced up at John, then at the rapidly scattering crewmembers behind the inner doors.

"Horseshit." This from a slim, tanned man with an expensive haircut, who had risen from a booth across from Emily. He made a show of rolling up his sleeve to display his gold watch. Looked at his equally perfect, equally poised wife, while addressing the room. "Our flight leaves in an hour. We're going to miss it."

"They have to rebook us," his wife replied, looking around. She tried to sound dismissive, but a shrill note had crept into her voice. "They have to. Hotel vouchers, free meals. This is unacceptable."

*Unacceptable.* The word caromed around the inside of Emily's skull, louder with every circle. Yet the passengers of Group Orange seemed to hang onto the elegant woman's words. They would accept anything they were told, Emily realized. In this untethered, uncertain moment, all they wanted was to be guided. Ushered back to normality, to the old familiar world of rules and simple logic.

She watched the empty corridor past the glass doors, only a few feet beyond the transparent barrier, but already out of reach. Already an entire world away.

***

By eleven, the tension in the Odysseus First Class Lounge was palpable. The chatter had died out, the arguments, the recriminations. Even the handsome yuppie-type and the belligerent fat couple were silent, as if unable to summon up any more spleen. Passengers stared at their phones, or at the floor, quiet in that strained way of people trying not to give in to panic.

John had his eyes closed, either dozing, or distancing himself from the situation. A family of four had broken out some kind of card game and was keeping up a pretense of play, the mother staring glassily at her hand, the father shuffling and reshuffling listlessly. Emily thought about the other passengers, the ones still in their cabins and suites, imagined them waiting anxiously for another utterance from the speaker system. Clueless and alone. At least here there was comfort in numbers, or there should be.

She started typing another text to Joanie, then couldn't stand the atmosphere anymore. Instead, she got up and walked out on the promenade deck, the outer doors parting silently before her. Gulls wheeled and screeched overhead, the sun already hot enough to burn, even in the shade. Past the railing, the dock was no longer empty.

A vehicle had pulled up to the ship's berth. It looked like a truck and hauled behind it a metallic gray trailer the size of a train car. *Probably a gas tanker*, she thought, *big enough to refuel the huge ship*. Then she remembered that the refueling had been completed hours ago, before anyone had been allowed to disembark. Emily leaned over, wishing she hadn't packed her bifocals. There was a symbol on the side of the truck's trailer, or tank, but she couldn't make it out.

She watched the vehicle crawl forward and halt more or less directly under her feet. It had an opening in the middle, a ring at least seven feet tall, although it was hard to tell from this angle. The terminal building behind the truck looked dead, all lights off, the doors closed. Surely it couldn't be closed this early in the day: four groups of passengers had already gotten off. A long hose snaked behind the truck, vanished into a thicket of

11

mobile fences.

There was activity further down the dock, figures moving behind what looked like a pile of sandbags. Squat and slow, too bulky to be people. Emily squinted, but the details remained blurry, the faces no more than dark circles.

Odd. It had not been raining, but the concrete of the dock glistened wet.

A great shapeless terror crested over Emily, threatening to overwhelm her. It was no particular realization, no single thing she had seen, but all of them taken together. She hurried back inside, the doors snapping shut with a noise that somehow sounded final.

***

"On behalf of the Company, we would like to extend our apologies." The ship's captain stood behind the inner doors, his white hat under his arm, his uniform sporting razor-sharp creases. "The problem has been resolved. The port authorities have informed me that we'll have you off this boat within the next half hour. Preparations are already underway."

"Why are we still here?" said a slender man with thinning hair, pushing his glasses up his nose. Flustered by the crowd's attention, he blushed and stepped back instinctively, found his way blocked by the fat couple, their faces wearing twin scowls of righteous indignation.

"A minor holdup with paperwork," the captain

said. His voice sounded just the way it had over the speaker, the remarks carefully scripted and delivered, and he was smiling, but only with the lower half of his face. "Nothing serious. Complimentary vouchers will be made available…"

"You're not telling us everything." The fat man with the red fishing cap pushed his way to the door. Steam and spittle misted the glass. "What kind of holdup? It's the virus, isn't it?" He spread his arms out, turned to his audience. "The bug. They think someone here's got it."

A roar of protest went up, drowning out the captain's response. Emily was shoved aside as bodies swarmed forward: palms struck the barrier lightly, as if testing its resistance, then harder. Someone went down in a flail of arms. A woman screamed; a child started crying.

"Folks, I'm going to have to ask you to calm down." The captain wasn't smiling anymore. "That's all the information we have to share right now. We'll keep you abreast of any new developments."

Either the change in his tone did the trick, or the realization that the doors would not open. One by one, the passengers dispersed, looking confused and embarrassed by the collective outburst.

Even the pink-faced man seemed beaten. "Open this door," he said, but instead of angry he now sounded petulant. Eventually he sat back down next to his wife, grumbling.

"They can't keep us in here," the supermom said from the back of the lounge. "Not with kids. No water, no bathroom."

Someone's fingers grazed Emily's shoulder. She turned round. John was holding his phone out to her, staring at it as though he'd forgotten how to use it. "I can't get through to Joanie," he said, and his voice sounded tired, old. "Not even to voicemail. There's no signal."

"It'll work when we get off the boat," Emily said, more to reassure herself than her husband. Phones were supposed to work; the lights were supposed to come on when you flipped the switch; airplanes to take off and land as scheduled. That was the way things had been seven days ago, and there was no reason to think otherwise.

The bleached blonde must have overheard them. She maneuvered her bulk over the creaking armrest, wearing an expression, both inquisitive and solicitous, that Emily knew well and disliked intensely. "Can't get through to your kid? The lines aren't working anymore."

"We got two," her pink-faced husband said, mopping his brow. "Up in Vermont. Moved there right after college. They're both into skiing."

"Ours is in San Diego," John said, before Emily could nudge him silent. "We've been calling her all day. Nothing."

"Isn't that place locked down?" All at once the blonde seemed eager to distance herself. "Didn't you hear? They sent the army in last night. No one's getting in or out."

"It's the damned Chinese," her husband said. "We send them our jobs, they send us back germs.

All the while our so-called government does nothing. Won't surprise me if this is deliberate. Some kind of attack."

The mother-of-two dropped her cards, stared at the fat man. "You're not serious," she said, glancing nervously at her husband, who looked irritated at no one in particular. "You can't be serious."

"We're not under attack," said a tall, white-haired man sitting across from the family. He looked up from the book he'd been reading, smiled at the children. "Just a delay getting into port, people. These things happen. We'll be all right."

But all Emily could think about were the darkened windows of the terminal, the strange truck parked next to the cruise ship.

When she sidled next to John, he patted her hand absently. "It can't be because of the bug," he said, continuing some inner monologue out loud. "It's no worse than the flu."

"What did you see when you went outside?" It took Emily a moment to realize that the fat man was addressing her. "What's down on the dock?"

Emily was taken aback by the sudden ferocity in his voice. Even more taken aback when other faces turned in her direction. Not to intervene, to tell her interrogator to shut up, but avidly expecting a response. She wanted to tell the asshole to mind his own business, and worse, but the touch of all those eyes sapped her resolve. "Nothing," she said, hating how weak her voice sounded. "It's just the dock."

It was wrong, what she said, the way she said it. The way she held back -- about the truck, about the absence of lights, the barricades, if that's what they were, being built in the distance. When they found out, she would look guilty, complicit in what was happening. But she'd blurted it out, and the moment had slipped away.

"You sure took your time looking at nothing," the blonde said, with a suspicious smirk. Emily felt John tense up next to her, felt anger flush her cheeks.

"Take a look for yourselves, if you don't believe me."

"We intend to," the fat man said, glancing around the room triumphantly. With an air of injured dignity, he got up and waddled over to the outer doors. Nothing happened. He waved his pink arms over his head, at the black eye of the motion sensor. Still nothing. The fat man turned back to the passengers, his expression a mix of confusion and anger.

"We need everyone back in their seats." There was no chime leading into the announcement this time, no apologetic note. The voice erupted from the speakers, harsh and flat, brooking no argument. "Please comply with the offboarding security protocol. Remain seated until instructed otherwise."

The fat man gazed at the speakers wide-eyed. Without a word, he shuffled back to his seat, head downcast like he was examining the plush carpet. Somehow his surrender was the most frightening thing Emily had witnessed all morning. She looked from face to face, trying to find a familiar set of features, recognize the happy, relaxed tourists she'd shared the ship with until a few hours ago, finding none. A cold fist squeezed her stomach until she felt lightheaded.

The well-dressed yuppie approached the inner door, slapped his palm against the glass. "I want to speak to someone in charge," he said, although Emily couldn't see anyone standing there. "We're not animals. You can't keep us in here. Open this door and let us out."

Two figures descended the staircase. The yuppie took an involuntary step back, allowing Emily an unimpeded view of the corridor. Neither of the new arrivals were ship's officers, nor service staff: that much was immediately apparent. Bloated and shapeless, their bodies blocked the narrow passage. There was something wrong with their faces.

Masks. They were wearing masks, and bulky biohazard suits, like scientists in an apocalypse movie. The same masks she'd seen from the ship's deck.

"Everything is in order, folks." The voice boomed overhead again, making an effort to sound agreeable and not doing a very good job of it. "This is just a precaution. For your own safety. Good news is, we're cleared to disembark. The gangway is being lowered as we speak."

"Did you see that?" John was fiddling with his glasses, mouth half open. "Who were those people? What's going on here?"

Emily shook her head. The suited shapes continued down to the lower level, disappearing from sight. She tried to recall the ship's plan, what was down there. Staff quarters, she was pretty sure, and engineering. It didn't bear thinking about. None of it did.

"You were outside," the fat blonde said to her, her small eyes crinkled and cruel. "When it happened. Before they closed the doors."

A babble of voices rose up around Emily, some wrathful, others frightened. She could feel the eyes on her again, a psychic wave of suspicion, of dislike, of fear of the unknown. But all those emotions were directed at the outside. Right now, she was reachable, she was the known. Unlike the officers who hid behind glass, unlike the masked, suited men, she could be confronted, spat at, hurt.

"Don't you touch my wife." John's voice traveled to her from a distance. She saw his face, red with fury, fists clenched.

"We have the right to know," the fat man said, almost prissily. "They're not telling us what it is."

"She doesn't know any more than we do." John looked at the white-haired man who had sounded so calm earlier. He wanted help, an ally in the rising tide of panic. The man looked away, seemed to shrink into himself. Vanished behind a wall of hard, identical faces, jaws set, mouths compressed into thin lines. No one had stepped forward to join in the accusations, Emily noticed, but it was only a matter of time. Even those who kept out of it seemed to approve.

"Oh, my God." The yuppie's wife rushed to the outer doors, pressed her face to the glass. "This can't be happening," she said in a small, strained voice.

The crowd crammed around her. A vast movement, like the ship itself had shifted underfoot. Everyone talking at once, the chatter edged with hysteria.

"What is that thing?" supermom said, her squalling baby forgotten.

Left alone, Emily couldn't see what was happening on the deck. But the commotion inside the ship caught her attention. A flash of white, a man in a shirt and little else, running up the stairs from belowdecks. His motions jerky and frantic, features distorted by terror. He almost made it to the door when he was seized by gloved hands and dragged back, white shirt tumbling down the staircase. She couldn't be sure, but she thought she heard distant screams and a noise like firecrackers, muffled by the glass.

The lights in the corridor cut out.

Weak-kneed, Emily collapsed onto the nearest chair. Her thoughts trickled slowly, like molasses. Through the gathered bodies, she could see movement out on the deck, right outside the lounge. A group of suited figures assembling something that looked like a huge tube. A robotic arm telescoped from below, pulled the structure upright. The suited crew manipulated the edges of the tube over the door, sealing off the lounge.

"Ladies and gentlemen." The disembodied voice cut through the sudden silence. "Please remain calm."

Fluorescent lights lit up the interior of the tube.

A tunnel, like the gullet of an immense plastic worm.

"Please form an orderly line," the voice said. "There was a disturbance on board, but it has been handled. Your safety is our foremost concern. When the doors open, please proceed down the tunnel. You have been cleared for entry. Mind your step and use the railing. Above all, do not panic."

John's hand was on her shoulder, squeezing too hard. Yet Emily welcomed its presence. At least she wouldn't be alone in the awful bright tunnel, the opening that matched the one in the side of the big trailer.

Doors slid open and the passengers moved forward, calm, as if hypnotized. Emily had time to wonder what had happened to Joanie. Whether the tunnel had been the last thing her daughter had seen. Then she let her thoughts dissolve.

It was almost over. They would walk out into a hot, sunny Florida day. Taxis would be running, the flights would be on time. She would call Joanie and bicker halfheartedly, make one more pitch to bring her home.

She took John's hand in hers, without meeting his eyes, and stepped into the tunnel.

## The Word

## Eric Thomas

My name is Dr. Josslyn Seward. I work with an organization known as Operation Fallen Tower as a Chief Medical Officer for Subject 1-373. I, and soon the entire facility, have been compromised. The Word is not what they've told you it is.

The artifact, what most of the world, almost all of them converts, knew as The Word, had been discovered a year ago in ancient Babylon. It was at first considered a relatively mundane tablet containing illegible script; upon closer examination it was discovered that the markings shared characteristics of Sumerian, Babylonian, Assyrian, Amorite, and even Aramaic script all mixed together into a single word. A linguist affiliated with the University of Memphis specializing in the ancient languages of what is now modern-day Iraq, Dr. Tamara Taylor, was tasked to assist in analyzing the script on the tablet by the request of an Iraqi linguist working out of the University of Iraq, Dr. Jermal Alkhadam. They, alongside a team of specialists consisting of other talented linguists, anthropologists, geologists, and philologists, a few being fellow university teachers from Iraq, the UK, and the United States, and most being doctoral students and interns working on their bachelor's degrees simultaneously, studied the tablet for six months, during which they gave the tablet the unofficial nickname "the Babel tablet." Until three months ago, everything had been kosher, with updates being made by the research team with the utmost expediency; and then they disappeared without a trace, taking every bit of research, assumed, and officially catalogued and shared with their respective institutions, including the Babel tablet.

Not a single word from the researchers had been heard by their employers, family, or friends for two to three weeks. And then an untraceable stream on the Deep Web began broadcasting 24/7 from an unknown location. It featured the Babel team dressed in ceremonial garbs that mimicked the religious aesthetic of ancient Mesopotamia crudely standing in a semi-circle, with Alkhadam and Taylor standing upon a platform in the middle of the team. All of them faced the camera, the members stationed below the two head researchers were playing equally make-shift, silvery flute-like instruments playing in a reedy orchestra that screamed and whined at disparate harmonies and melodies; meanwhile, Alkhadam and Taylor spoke in tongues that shouldn't have been understandable to anyone, given that it sounded like a garbled gumbo of five different languages. While that was the case at first, the more viewers watched and listened to the stream, the more they claimed to understand the gibberish. What they claimed to hear was perfect, coherent sentences in their respective languages, but when they were asked what they heard, they couldn't recall. The answer shared by all was that it was an incredibly subjective experience and that one needed to witness it for themselves.

Even stranger, as the stream began to garner hundreds of viewers, in our best estimation of events, they seemed to quit their lives entirely and had become utterly obsessed with this stream, which, after a month, still couldn't be traced by the most powerful intelligence and military organizations in the world. They all seemed to hear a similar message that they themselves couldn't convey: one of unity, one of breaking down all borders and barriers, cultural, military, governmental, linguistic, all of them. At first, most of the world had considered them a cult that had stolen what was the most significant historical artifact to be discovered in the last 200 years. Strangely, this framework didn't hold up, with many, progressing to thousands over a week, proclaiming to be converts of this gracious message of beautiful unity of humankind. From average civilians to celebrities, from religious apologists, priests, preachers, and local religious leaders to major leaders in those religions, from local capitalizing politicians to world leaders trying to catch the wave, all of them eventually became true-blue believers in the message of what had initially become known as the "Cult of Babel."

The numbers of converts became hundreds of

thousands and in no time at all millions. Movements and demonstrations were held throughout the world, whether it was in the United States or even in countries who held the idea of free speech as governmentally pernicious, such as North Korea, China, and Russia. All of them were peaceful, despite how in the latter countries and those like them violence had been swiftly laid upon the participants and their families. Despite this, they still organized and preached the message of unity of peoples, going as far as to denounce their own countries and renounce their citizenship. According to the FBI and NSA, who had attempted to spy and see a common thread between the believers, of which they found no single line of communication between the professed followers of the Cult of Babel, there wasn't any evidence of a structured, organized religion. There wasn't a single leader in the entire movement. Not even the inner circle of the cult streaming were considered leaders. They, just like everybody else, were merely thought of as messengers of what they referred to as "The Word". No matter what push-back they received across the globe, the ostensibly headless movement were like ants; single-minded and devoid of individual purpose and will, they seemed to move according to an inner instinct that was agreeable to the whole. The only discernable agenda shared amongst the fast-growing multitudes was the ideal of the pursuit and complete and total unity amongst humankind. Multiple interactions with the members of the Cult said that they consented to the will of a presence that seemed to afflict those exposed to The Word. They had no singular name for this entity and no origin for it, claiming that it had always existed, many making these claims under the guise of the entity.

The movement culminated when, without any provocation that anyone else could see or make sense of, every single convert, it's believed, flew and sailed, legally and otherwise, to Baghdad. The tumultuous city was overrun, practically invaded, and the government sent their military in full force. The world held their breath, with many world leaders warning the Iraqi government of the consequences of firing upon their respective expatriates while also trying to offer support against the Cult's actions, using this as an example as to their pernicious nature. The stand-off lasted for a whole two weeks before the President and the leaders of the Iraqi military met with the Cult. Talks lasted for five hours before they came out. The President then appeared with the elected spokesmen of the Cult on international television, announcing that not only would this massive transplantation not be disturbed but would be *encouraged*, and that now was the time of humanity's unitization and consequent ascension before allowing the members of the Cult to speak. All threats of violence from extremist organizations and legitimate military apparatus' within Iraq, and soon the entire Middle East, was quelled. Instead, millions more in Iraq, including most of the military, abandoned their lives to follow the Cult into the desert, where the ancient ruins of Babylon were located. That's when they began to build. Not a tower to reach the heavens, but a new city-state, open to all who were open to all, that stretched outside of Baghdad and stretched until it covered Iran.

Once they realized how dire this "infection", as they came to see it, was, many governments, even those that preached the value of free speech, didn't stop at spying on the faithful; they outright sought to block the Deep Web stream and any auxiliary outlet from which it could be seen from the Internet. When they couldn't accomplish anything beyond policing the surface of the Internet, they cracked down on the equipment people used to access the Deep Web. The banning of talks of The Word or the Cult of Babel brought about a virtual police state. Those in power were right to be afraid. This philosophy, this "Word", did what no other religion, politics, philosophy, science, whatever one could think of that attempted to bring the world together under one peaceful umbrella, could. It was changing people's perspectives and it was virulent, using people changed by The Word as a vector, like flies spreading diseases. All under the auspices of some sort of intelligence that couldn't be seen, touched, or hurt. The only people who seemed immune to The Word were those who vehemently resisted it, giving many the notion that it was all a consenting act and not the global takeover they were being told it was. But still it continues to grow exponentially and those opposed to it grew as fanatical—and violent—in turn.

This is how we, those at Operation Fallen Tower, have come to be where we are. Even with the grip the government had on the population's access to information, there would still be an *infection* (words such as "convert", or "conversion" were strictly relegated to what the government considered to be a "legitimate religious nature") would pop up here and there. Thanks to the immunity, though, those of us who still resist are able to analyze them. The infected would be quarantined away from the rest of society indefinitely (or permanently; depending on if you knew whether or not they were dead) in order to study The Word's effect on people. Initially, conversation was considered an optimum tool of analysis, with only the most strong-willed of interrogators allowed to interact with the subjects. That, however, didn't go as planned.

***

When talking to a subject afflicted with The Word, we have concurred that, while the individual is comparatively the same as he or she was before infection, there lies a curious undercurrent within the subject—something akin to an alien intelligence, as mentioned before. Each subject talks of a certain shared experience of travelling through the cosmos and time, being outside as well as inside of it. While these were formerly thought of as the inane ramblings of people with broken, zealous minds, over time each subject, when prodded, had shared knowledge of some sort concerning the fabric of reality that they would have no typical reason for knowing. Say, a carpenter being able to accurately describe the function of dark matter mathematically. Further conversation reveals that this... *entity* is aware and exists as a shared experience with the host. It has also alluded to even further knowledge that not even we as a species understand but refuses to tell us. We are confident that this is one entity, spreading across the entirety of the Cult and not several because every time a subject is terminated, another one will remember exactly what had happened to the last. It describes itself as not being alive in the conventional sense and has only existed for as long as "observers" such as we have existed but remains unknown to a species until a certain threshold is crossed. Not technologically, culturally, or in any way that can be objectively measured as progress for a civilization and/or species. However, it speaks of a mental one. Once that threshold is crossed, there is no going back. It claims it is not malicious, it is natural and necessary. It is *inevitable*. Subject was the last one to be interviewed and was terminated shortly after the end of the interrogation.

After the final interrogation, the SOP changed. The last subject, Subject 1-373, not only had her tongue cut out, but she also had her teeth removed, her mouth was always covered unless it was to feed her through a sophisticated tube that keeps her from utilizing her mouth at all, and she was also lobotomized in order to maintain the safest possible environment for our research team. Our mission was not to interview her or the entity, but to simply perform brain scans—before and after it is excised. The ethical strictures have been noted and loosened in this experiment by the United States government. At the present moment, The Word has reportedly infected almost three quarters of the entire planet. Again, this thing was dug out of the ground not even a year ago. Our government is afraid that we are looking not only down the barrel of a shotgun from a national perspective, but that of a species. We will begin with a CT scan of the subject's brain in order to ascertain whether or not the structure has had any changes, substantial or minor, in any way since the emergence of the entity; afterwards, we will perform an EEG-fMRI. Once all necessary data is collected, subject will be euthanized so we can study the brain more directly.

***

As soon as a subject arrives, they have no name. Subject 1-373 was no different. That didn't stop me from imagining what I would call them by; *she* looked like a Marie. She had black hair and pale skin that contrasted strongly with the pitch of her hair. Her pigment was marble-esque. Whether that was her natural coloration or because she hadn't been exposed to sunlight for months and had been fed the most basic nutrients since she was quarantined, I hadn't the faintest. She had soft blue eyes that looked like light blue resin paint spread over well varnished oak. The strangest thing about her, about all of the subjects, really, is how the light never went out of their eyes. I don't know if that was the case after they were terminated, but many of them had spent months here and it must have occurred to them that they would never be going home. They still had a strange life in their eyes, which we chocked to the entity that was residing within them. Personally, though, of which I was always remiss to admit, but it felt like there was more to it than that; at least, that was the thought that leaked into my thoughts at night. Those unwanted thoughts and reminders of their humanity, it struck me and others *hard*. It made me hate them. I despised how compliant and happy they seemed to be despite everything we had been forced to do to them. I saw not only forgiveness in their goddamned eyes, but also empathy. Like we were the bad guys, but they had that self-righteous they-know-not-what-they-do look of sympathy. It was *them* that was destroying *our* world, not the other way around. They, under the influence of this "entity" have done irreparable damage to society. So much so that even though I dutifully applied myself to the mission, I had doubts that we could ever go back to what humanity was before The Word. I kept telling myself, 'They're not human. Not really. Not anymore. At best, they're collaborators and at worst they're shells for an alien bent on destroying our way of life.' No matter how content they looked, no matter how innocent, no matter how young or old, they only had one use now and that was to stop this global pandemic. No matter how many it took. At the time, I would gladly cut into every single one until I found what missing puzzle piece contained our salvation.

She was restrained via straitjacket, tightened as much as possible. No evidence suggested that The Word could be transmitted via physical touch—in fact, not a single member of staff that had handled a subject, which was practically all of them, with their bare hands had been affected. Whenever a subject needed to be physically manipulated, we wore these dreadful hazmat suits that perturbed claustrophobic feelings in me. But given the aforementioned infected interrogator, the oversight committee wasn't taking any chances. Her legs were wrapped in thick white sheets and wrapped with three black belts. Still, she had that look of peace in her eyes. *Fucking freak,* I thought. Darius, the CT scanner technician stepped inside of the room alongside Frank, all three of us dressed in a hazmat suits.

"Let's roll," he said. I got up and followed them to the room where her x-rays would be taken. Dr. Strig was standing inside of his office, door ajar. "Hey, doc, we're starting the scans now."

"Finally, it's been four hours. Let's get this over with." Just because this operation had little to no regulations besides the oversight committee's constantly barking up everyone's tree, that didn't mean that it didn't fall under the arm of the government. Therefore, it had taken an ungodly amount of time to prep all the machines and the subject—all of which should have taken, at most, thirty minutes to an hour. All measures and precautions needed to be taken account of in order to assure some sort of successful venture. They would need to take her out of her restraints in order to take the x-rays. It took around fifteen minutes before they were done, and the girl was returned to her wheelchair and the restraints that looked like torturous vestments on a martyr mired in righteous suffering.

***

"Okay, Frank, let's take her to Nyomi next." Nyomi was the MRI tech who operated the fMRI-EEG. When we got to the MRI room, Nyomi was throwing a ball against a wall, catching it absentmindedly. She hadn't noticed that we had come in until I cleared my throat. She didn't jump but paused for a moment after catching the ball before swinging around in her swivel chair.

"Y'all finally ready?"

"More than," I replied. Frank took her to the fMRI-EEG scanner. Nyomi, in a hazmat suit of her own, covered the subject in the electric nodes. The fMRI-EEG would take fifty-five minutes.

"What do you think we'll find?" Nyomi asked.

"Not sure, but given the existence of The Entity, there should be some form of overlap on her brain waves," I replied.

"What's the big idea?"

"What do you mean?"

"I mean, what are we going to do if we find some kind of "overlap" or whatever?"

"Don't you work here?" I asked, a bit annoyed. I was fully mission-oriented and small talk was something I rarely engaged in; however, Nyomi was not only, unfortunately for me at the time, personable, but also a needy conversationalist.

"C'mon, Dr. Seward, I just want to pick your brain. You're her doctor. You can't tell me that you haven't had any ideas?"

"I try not to have any ideas until I have hard data in my hand. That way, I'm not too invested in any one idea. I, *we*, need a *direction*. This situation is far too delicate; it requires our best."

At this, Nyomi blew her breath, dismayed by my constant social deflections. After a few moments passed, she asked, "But it couldn't really hurt, don't you think? Aren't you supposed to be thinking about the threat all the time? You can't not have had any thoughts about this."

At this, I pinched the bridge of my nose. "Okay. There is… *one* thought I've had."

Nyomi brightened, and her ears perceptibly lifted. "Go on," she teased.

"I think… I think that…" I hated talking about my thoughts on the spot. It seemed tedious and I felt it made me look incredibly unprofessional; I needed notes, examples, numbers in front of me so I could articulate what was basically a cognitive blob in my head. Nyomi didn't seem to care how uncomfortable this made me. "I think that since there *is* an intelligence that clings onto the infected, much like Subject 1-373, that it's parasitic in nature. While it isn't physically detectable, therefore making it impossible to cut out like a tumor, it could possibly feed or depend on the neurons and the way that they fire in the brain."

"And... what would we do about that? It's basically an abstract thought. How do we destroy a thought?"

"You understand that most people who hear The Word change, almost immediately, right?"

"Yeah, it's why I don't have an uncle anymore." Nyomi was also one to overshare and joke in order to cope. To this day it has struck me as a big mistake bringing someone this extroverted and socially outgoing onto a secret government project that held the fate of the world in the balance, no matter how great her work was.

"Sure. Now, while we can't outright eliminate conscious thoughts," *Yet*, I thought, "we may be able to reverse the effect. I believe that it mostly has to do with the sound. However, then a problem arises: the person. The reception of The Word requires the person to be mentally open to its influence."

"But if we can't just control people's thoughts, what do we do?"

I looked her in the eyes, "It will take some... extreme convincing, at the present moment. And that's if my hypothesis is correct."

"Oh," Nyomi said.

"Yep. I believe that we'll need to devise some kind of exposure therapy so that we can kill this parasite. Person by person." A beep sounded off.

"Great, we are officially done. And *I* can go

home," Nyomi cheered, committing to her task with a renewed vitality you see when people have one more thing keeping them from getting in their car and burning tire on their way out. The subject, *Marie*, was back in her chair and wheeled out. I was thankful for the end of the tests as well. The rubber sticking to my skin felt suffocating, like I had been packaged. It's an ironic feeling to have when you're responsible for examining a living thing, trapped beyond belief.

***

Marie was placed in her cell—a barren blue room where she would sit in her chair, still restrained, surrounded by thick rubber walls that were soft enough to bash your head against without killing yourself but hard enough to knock even the most hard-headed case out if they tried. I was the only one left, save for security that patrolled the perimeter and the few that had access to walk the inside of the facility. Given how easily the infected acquiesced to our demands, security was lax - it's only function being for anyone who was exposed to The Word so that they can be locked away for study. Sitting down at my desk, I accessed my government email to retrieve the results of the CT scan and fMRI-EEG.

As I suspected, the CT scan was normal. The specimen was frightening; an ethereal being that existed in the thoughts of the host, subsisting off their brain activity. It's not that it didn't offer benefits of its own, as it more than, how you might say, put the host at "ease". Interviews with the infected, while failures ultimately, they did provide interesting tidbits of information. The infected, as mentioned before, become apathetic to things like money, family, nation, anything that ties them to their former lives. Not even the bond of parenthood can keep them grounded. Not even subtleties such as the innate preference for one's one race, ethnicity, gender, or sex registered in their minds anymore. They put the identity of the whole infection before themselves and as a consequence they lost themselves *entirely*. That's what terrified me, the loss of individuality. Disappearing into a void, where I lost control. Peace, love, that meant nothing if people couldn't be themselves.

I clicked the imbedded file containing the fMRI-EEG results. I read them. And they didn't register as regular brain waves. They were all over the place, sporadically shooting in angles that didn't make any sense… until I looked closer. Until I *perceived* what I was reading. The scans were forming repeated angles and shapes… it looked like a language I couldn't remember learning but knew that deep within my soul was as compatible to me as my own DNA. As I read, there was fear and hesitation at first. My life, my attachments, flashed before my eyes. My parents. My brother. My niece. My friends. My dog. Everything. And then something very curious happened: they didn't fall away. Instead, they fell into place in a picture that was bigger than my life, bigger than the lives of each and every human being on this Earth. Bigger than the solar system, galaxy, bigger than the universe itself. It didn't feel like nothing mattered, it felt like meaningless boundaries and divisions didn't matter anymore. I saw my life in the stars and my death in the atoms that made up the flowers on my future grave. I saw agony and love inversely and together; all of the emotions on the spectrum of experience. I saw the numbers that made up the soul as it spoke in rewritten code.

I hadn't noticed the tears that streamed down my face as I became possessed but, unlike what I had thought, I was still here. I was still me, but my *perspective* had changed. It wasn't all about me or what I thought mattered to me. It was like I was all of us, and all of us were me. I would never be alone again, not even when my time had come and gone. I would never end; every part of me would stretch their legs throughout reality, bringing impossible beauty into existence. I saw lifetimes in seconds and atoms that took eternity to build just to vanish. I read and my hate, anger, and sadness fell away; though they would exist with me so long as I or life itself lived, I feel like I could carry them and more. I was stronger than any human that had ever existed because I had entered life instead of simply allowing it to enter me. I wasn't just Josslyn P. Seward. I wasn't *just* human. I was an *idea*. And *we* became *alive*.

## Return to Source

### S.G. Kubrak

"Hey, man. I said don't move!" he yelled at me, holding the .45 in front of him, slapping the magazine into the gun. His hands shook.

I stood back and held my hands up in front of me, palms forward showing him that I wasn't a threat. Or at least I hoped it showed him that.

"Look, I can talk right? My skin isn't that bone-white color. I can move just as fast as you can." I waved my hands in front of my face, and enunciated every word clearly, not like the abominations that slurred that phrase over and over, shambling around the building.

"That don't mean shit, you could still be one of them, they might have just assimilated you and you are trying to get to me!" He spat out his words, then pulled the top of the .45 back, loading a bullet into the chamber.

I did my best to think as quickly as I could, the adrenaline pumping so hard I was just reacting and not thinking.

He started firing.

I dropped to the floor and covered my ears. He wasn't shooting at me, or I'd be dead.

"Re-turn to sssssss…" the abomination hissed as it sank to the floor, purple blood spurting in all directions.

I held my ears until the gunfire stopped. Five rounds, more than was needed. He was reacting too.

"Fine," he said, popping out the magazine and slamming in a new one.

The body of the abomination continued to gurgle out the phrase they all uttered, "Re-turn to source," it repeated gently, almost a whisper.

"I wish they'd stop saying that!" he hissed then shot the corpse two more times, yet it continued to repeat the phrase.

"C'mon, let's get out of here. I can't make them stop." His voice quavered.

We ran down the stark white hallway, passing the corpses of abominations, their twisted, inhuman faces staring at us as we ran by, all whispering, "Return to Source."

At the end of the dimly lit hallway, a silver door was left open and we quickly ran through it. He slammed it shut behind us.

The room was small, barely fifteen feet square. A ladder leading up to a stack of crates offered the only escape from the floor. It provided questionable protection from the shambling monsters.

"Okay, go up first, I am right behind you," he commanded. I looked over the top of the crates, barely larger than a bunkbed. I had no idea how he thought the two of us were going to fit up there.

"Hey, I don't think…" I started, until his fist hit me in the side of the head. I hauled back my own fist, ready to return the favor, and found myself staring into the barrel of the .45.

"I ain't playing with you asshole," he said calmly.

I shook my head and backed off, then headed for the ladder. A plaintive mew called down from the crates.

A kitten?

I stepped up on the first rung and looked across. There in a clear plastic bucket was a stark white kitten. It circled around, not focusing on where it was going, as if it were unaware of anything. It mewed incessantly.

"Jesus, now it's getting cats?" he hissed, and pushed me off the ladder to look into the bucket.

I swear, if he didn't have that gun…

Through the side of the bucket, I could see the kitten shaking as it circled, its condition deteriorating until it curled into a ball, mewing continually. "Dude, it's in pain, maybe you should…" More death was not something I wanted, but the cat was suffering and the last thing any of us needed was more pain.

"Yeah," he said. He aimed and fired, three times.

I turned away, opening the door he had just slammed shut. The bucket with the kitten carcass sailed past my head and clanged onto the floor.

"Good riddance," he said, reaching around me and slamming the door shut again. Then he pointed the gun back at me. "Okay, back up."

With little choice I climbed back up to the top of the crates where the snow-white kitten had erstwhile been.

"Those bastards will stop at nothing. Using an innocent cat to try to assimilate us. Who do they think they are?" He spoke into the air. I presumed it was rhetorical and didn't answer. Then his fist landed in my ribs.

"I said, who do they think they are?" he asked.

"Monsters?" I spat back at him, not hiding my anger.

"Fucking monsters. Yep."

He put the gun down and started reloading the magazines with rounds from a small box, the bullets inches from my face.

"Uh, firearm discipline?" I asked.

He racked the gun next to my head. "Yep, the discipline is that I do what I want, and you shut up."

Who was I safer with? My anger was interrupted by a knock at the door.

"Hey. In there. Open up," a male voice called through the door, it sounded familiar to me.

"Who the fuck is it?" he yelled, pointing the gun at the door, then slid himself off the crates and landed softly on the floor. As crazy as he was, he knew what he was doing - I didn't hear him at all.

"Please, we're trying to get away from them, we're one of you," the voice implored.

"Please!" another voice, female, begged.

He turned and pointed two fingers at me, then at the door. He grabbed the knob as I steeled myself to see as much as I could when he swung it open.

The door opened so quickly I could barely make out what was going on at first or what I was seeing. A man and a woman stood there, their faces and clothes stark white. But not assimilated, just… painted. Behind the two of them an abomination shuffled, its body a featureless humanoid with no gender, as if it were a mannequin; just enough for the impression of a human but not detailed. Its head was in the shape of a horse, its long snout jutted out from the rest of the body by a foot or more. The lifeless eyes glowed purple.

He instantly slammed the door, trapping them outside with it.

"Noah! Please let us in! They are coming!" the male screamed desperately.

That was his name. Why didn't I know that?

Noah put his foot against the bottom of the door, bracing it to keep it closed.

"Ain't tricking me!" he said and shook his head.

"Noah! DON'T!" the man yelled again, followed by both of them screaming then falling silent.

"Not gonna trick me," he said, then opened the door again, holding the gun in front of him.

The couple stood with their backs to us,

transfixed on the abomination that embraced them with its arms. White and blue tendrils curled out from its eyes, plunging into the couple's faces. Pulsing and writhing, their heads shook as the projections squirmed throughout their skulls.

"Re-turn to source," they whispered in unison with the horse-faced abomination.

"Damnit," Noah swore, and emptied the entire magazine into the trio. Their bodies fell in a shower of purple blood. He slammed the door closed.

"Goddamn it!" he yelled. "Almost got me! Almost fucking got me!"

He turned back into the room, his eyes wide. "We ain't gonna let them get us, right? RIGHT?"

I nodded emphatically, dumbfounded at the violence.

Noah flipped up the green blanket that had been covering all the crates, every wooden box read "Ammunition", stenciled in white.

Where the hell are we?

He opened a crate, pulled out a smaller box of bullets, and proceeded to reload the two magazines he had been trading back and forth.

"See, the way I look at it, they could be coming at us forever here." He tapped on another box. "These are just bullets though, no food, so…" He turned to look at me.

"No, I ain't gonna eat ya, but we need food, and you gotta earn your keep. So, take this." He reached into his thigh pocket and pulled out a six-inch blackjack. "You go back down that hall and turn right, there is a pantry. Get all the food you can carry and come back here."

My mind scrambled. "What? With those things out there? They'll catch me."

His eyes narrowed and held there for a minute; his gaze was withering. A moment later he smiled and laughed like he had just heard the funniest joke in human history.

"Nah, just fuckin' with ya. We'll both go." He held up the gun and waved it around, with the safety off.

"Okay," I squeaked out.

Noah popped the door back open and looked around for movement. The bodies of the recently deceased abominations lay on the ground in front of the door, including the two painted white people he just shot. Purple blood oozed from the bullet wounds in their bodies. The horse faced abomination lay just beyond them, the lights out of its eyes, yet still muttering, "Re-turn to source."

"Now make sure they don't catch you, and don't make me kill you, man. You turn, I'll load you up, just like that cat," Noah warned, brandishing the gun again.

I nodded stupidly; it made no sense to argue with a crazy man with a gun. Looking around at the carnage, I knew he had no qualms about using it and would more than likely do as he promised.

We walked back down the hallway to where he

found me earlier. The wide room was featureless, its stark white walls offering no ornamentation, except the spattering of purple blood.

"I was looking for something, but I can't remember what it was. A closet or something. Had something important in it," I explained, trying to remember.

"Yeah, the pantry, dumbass. The first task in a crisis is to secure provisions. You don't know how long it will last."

I looked at him, his eyes fixed on me, but distant, like he was looking through me. I had no idea what was going through is mind. "No, that's not it," I said, more to get my brain on the right track than to explain myself.

"Whatever. Now turn that corner up ahead, then make a right. Keep that blackjack ready."

I held the bludgeon, completely unsure of how to properly use it except to bean someone over the head like hitting a dog with a newspaper after it took a shit on the Persian rug. Maybe it was really all I needed anyway.

We turned the corner and were assaulted by a chorus of "Re-turn to source." The walls seemed to come alive with abominations. All bone-white with no anatomy. Every one of them had a twisted head, some animal, some looking like plants, or writhing snakes. Nothing looked human.

"Shit! Run!" Noah screamed and opened fire, spraying the air with bullets, with complete disregard for me. I hit the ground and covered my head; that bastard didn't care if he hit me, I was on my own.

"I'll kill you! You get no mercy from me!" he screamed as he turned back down the hallway, firing over his shoulder. In one move he ejected the magazine, dropping it on the floor, and slammed in a new one. He continued to fire and run.

I huddled on the floor shivering and waiting to meet my fate. Noah's screams ended abruptly as he slammed the door shut behind him. The chorus grew louder.

"Re-turn to source... re-turn to source... re-turn..."

Then the chanting stopped. I peeked through my fingers at the bone-white feet surrounding me. I must be dead, or assimilated, or whatever you wanted to call it. I don't know why they were taking their time though, none of the other ones did.

I stood up, not understanding, and focused down the hallway past the grotesque abominations now standing like statues in some surrealist museum. They parted and flanked the walls, the ones that had faces turned toward the back, as the largest one I had ever seen turned the corner. Easily seven feet tall, it strode down the corridor, its movements surprisingly fluid. Again, anatomically featureless, its smooth body culminated in a horrific head, a stark-white human brain in a glass jar, clear fluid sloshing as it moved.

My eyes boggled at the image, I couldn't move, and the lights of the room seemed to darken, everything grew quiet save for my pounding heart and panicked breathing. The brain in the jar moved toward me, raising its tentacle covered hands. They shot toward my face with such speed I could not blink before my world went purple and then dark.

***

"Preston? Preston, can you hear me?"

The voice entered my consciousness from somewhere, I wasn't sure. It was female, and warm, someone who obviously cared about me. I tried to respond but couldn't. I didn't know how to speak - I knew I could, but I'd forgotten how.

"Preston, blink if you can understand me," the voice said again.

Blink? My eyes have to be open to do that don't they? Are my eyes open? Why can't I tell?

I tried to get my body to do anything at all instead of floating in the dark expanse it was in.

Yell. You can do that. Just yell.

I willed my body to scream, and I became conscious of a low groan coming from somewhere below me. Deep and guttural. My chest vibrated.

That was me! Good, keep doing that!

"Preston, come on, wake up. You can do it," the voice reassured, I heard others in the background urging 'Preston' on. I assumed it was me and pushed harder.

The guttural groan got louder, not a yell, but more like a vomit of sound that oozed out of my face and spilled down my cheeks.

"Good!" the voice congratulated. "He's coming around."

The world slowly slithered into focus. I was lying down, blue-white lights hung overhead illuminating everything in a sickly hue. I could smell antiseptic and rubber. My eyes blinked, each movement bringing pain.

"Okay Preston, just lie there, it will take a little while longer for the antitoxin to move through your system, you will feel prickly for a bit, and hot, don't worry your vitals are coming back strong. Be patient."

I tried nodding but wasn't sure if that was my head moving or my vision swimming.

The light suddenly got brighter; the person who was speaking must have moved away. Then it grew darker, and a different female voice addressed me.

"How many bullets does he have? Didn't you hear the drone calling you? We were trying to reach you with one of your drones." She was very perfunctory, almost cold.

Sitting up, my body screamed at me to stay still, every inch of verticality was a herculean effort. "Mmmm-mm. Maii… ddddroone?" I managed to garble out of my mouth.

"Yes, your drone. We put it in his office when

you distracted him. You don't remember running to tackle him, do you?"

That was news to me. I turned to the voice, a wild tangle of tentacles greeted me, spilling out of the jar filled with clear fluid. The brains were surely inside.

"Wh-why haavveeen… haven't you… assimi…" I stuttered, blinking feverishly and trying to get a clear look at the abomination before I was stripped of my individuality.

"Assim…? Assimilated? You think we are going to assimilate you?" the voice asked, incredulous. The other woman in the room laughed.

I squeezed my eyes as hard as I could and shook my head.

"He's still hallucinating, give him a minute," the first woman explained.

"Halucin… ate?" I asked, not bothering to open my eyes.

"Mr. Preston," the colder voice began. "You, like most of the staff of the lab, have been hallucinating as the result of a neurotoxin… incident. It was a level four emergency, the building locked down and you were on your way to coordinate with physical security when the toxin affected you as well."

"Moannsters… assimilating people… abominations." The words came a little easier.

"Preston, look at me. I'm not a monster."

I turned my face to her, but I was too scared to open my eyes.

"Preston, we need you to return to the security server and restart the systems. We can't get out of the building without someone reinitializing the source code."

"Return… to… source?" I asked, looking her in the face and straining my eyes, her curly brown hair draped over oversized glasses. Large brown eyes regarded me, blinking slowly.

"Painted people?" I asked, still unsure of who they were.

Her eyes narrowed. "I'm not sure what you mean."

"Painted people, all white. Not… abominations."

"Fascinating, you could tell who had security clearance. Probably reading the IDs. They were contractors. We couldn't get them into the lab before the building locked down. They were trapped in the support offices upstairs. They don't have access with their badges like we do."

She reached over onto her lapel and grabbed her ID lanyard; it read "Dr. Carolin Henderson."

"Gun and bullets. Lots of bullets," I explained, shaking my head, thinking back to how Noah mercilessly slaughtered them.

"He only has one box of bullets. We aren't set for an invasion here."

I shook my head, remembering vividly how many crates of ammo he literally sat on and watching him blow through rounds like he had an infinite supply.

"Preston," she continued, "he only has one box of ammo, we've been counting the rounds, he may have ten, fifteen at the most, it's why we swarmed him when we recovered you."

I looked across the lab, my eyes rapidly clearing as the antitoxin finally made it to my optic nerves, and saw the bodies piled up in the freezer, the window covered in frost.

"I'm sorry, I didn't realize… I couldn't…"

"It's okay," she reassured me. "You were under the influence of the toxin; you couldn't have known."

I looked her in the eyes, the oversized glasses enlarging them like an owl's. "The toxin, can't we just wait it out? Won't it get better, or… kill him?"

Dr. Henderson stood up and drew a deep breath. She explained slowly as if the words themselves were too painful to utter. "There is every reason to believe that the toxin will destroy the central nervous system. He'll die in agony. If we wait for it to kill him, that is premeditated murder. He'll go insane and claw his eyes out before he succumbs to fatigue or hunger."

"How do you know this?" I asked, standing up from the bed and surveying the room. Lab-coated techs treated the wounded, ran IVs, and checked their equipment. In the corner, two techs hovered over a rat in a cage. It twitched violently, vomiting purple blood, and screeching pitifully.

"That is ten times the dosage, the LD50 is quite

low. We don't have much time," she said looking away from the bone-white rat, purple blood oozing from its eyes. It went still.

I did some quick math. "Even with only one box, he's got enough bullets to kill all of us here. We can't just bum-rush him."

"No, we can't," responded the first woman who treated me, "but *they* can." She pointed to a box on the far side of the room. It was filled with playing card-sized four wheeled robots. "Your drones. The ones we use to move things around in the containment area. You can program them to distract him long enough."

"Long enough?" I asked, waiting for her, or my brain, to catch up. It did quickly. "Why do I have to be the one that sticks his neck out to take that lunatic on?"

I couldn't believe the words coming out of my mouth.

Don't you see the bodies, asshole?

I looked down at the woman who brought me back from the brink. The one who saved me from a horrible death by neurotoxin, or lead poisoning. Down. I looked down. I was the biggest person in the room by almost a foot, and easily fifty pounds. Who else was big enough to take on an armed security guard?

"Shit. I'm sorry. I'm not all here yet."

Dr. Henderson cocked her head to the side, gesturing to some of the other techs. They went into another room and within a minute returned with bottles of water and protein bars.

"Get started," she plainly stated.

Over the next fifteen minutes I reprogrammed the drones to move forward in a serpentine pattern, hoping to avoid the deadly aim of Noah. I downloaded the source re-initialization program onto a thumb drive that would activate as soon as I slammed it into a USB port. I tried not to focus on the fact that I was about to go back up against a man who was a toxin-induced paranoid psychotic… and me armed only with a blackjack and a dozen drones that would be mewing kittens to his addled mind. After checking and double checking, I knew the time had come.

"Is there any way you can cover me, or give me some kind of distraction?"

Dr. Henderson replied, "We only managed to sneak the drone in when he was looking around and found you, and then we lost Peters as he was trying to cure the contractors. I'm not risking another person."

Except me.

I grabbed the box of drones and put the thumb drive in my pocket, making sure it was deep enough that it wouldn't fall out, or break from a collision. In my other pocket I put an injection of antitoxin; it was spring loaded, like an EpiPen. I took a deep breath.

"Okay, let's get this done."

One of the techs opened the door out into the hallway, the rancid stench of the blood-soaked walls filled the air. It wasn't pure white like I remembered, but grey. Grey walls splattered with red blood, slowly turning black as it oxidized. The positive pressure vents pulled as much air as they could into the circulation system, running it through as much carbon filter and UV light as possible and then returning it slowly to the air. It sill reeked. The tech slid the box of drones behind me, hitting me in the back of the legs. I knew exactly where I needed to go, and with no one backing me up, I knew that I would be doing it all alone.

"Good luck," Dr. Henderson said. She smiled and shut the door behind me, bolting it closed.

Thanks.

The long hallway stretched on, making the turn into the main area, then from there the other hallway to the security office. I knew I made this exact trek before; it was the one that got me contaminated apparently, but I don't remember any of that. It must be retroactive amnesia. As a matter of fact, I don't remember too much anymore. Just images really, feelings. But I do remember how crazy Noah was, and I remember the "kitten".

I walked down, trying to be as silent as possible, but I knew full well that he could hear me coming. I hoped that the paranoid-psychotic rage that he was in kept him locked into the room until I could get to him. It bothered me at the thought of hoping that someone, with a pistol and a hair-trigger, stayed psychotic. The first turn down, the stench of blood and bodies was overpowering. Several times I wretched uncontrollably, desperate to stay on my feet and not succumb to nausea.

Turning again, I reached the hallway to the security office. It was darker than I remembered, as if he turned the lights off to conceal the entrance. Or shot them out, knowing him. I hoped Dr. Henderson was correct in her assessment of his ammo. Regardless though, he was a trained security officer and pretty crazy. I wasn't feeling completely confident in my ability to take him down, armed or not.

I knelt down and emptied the box of drones on the floor, setting them upright so that their wheels had good purchase. I rolled them back and forth like matchbox cars. I knew they would be fine; I was just delaying the inevitable. Then the inevitable arrived.

"Who the fuck? What are you doing out there?" Noah yelled through the door. My hands shook and I swallowed hard as I pulled out the switch to activate the drones.

"Is that you? They didn't get you, right?"

Don't say anything.

My hands shook so badly I had to hold the switch with two hands until I could press the activate button. When I did, the drones sprang to life and arranged themselves in neat rows, moving slowly toward the other end of the hallway.

"Kittens again? What the fuck is wrong with you?"

I heard the door unbolt, and I dove for cover out of the hallway as a bullet ricocheted off the wall next to my head.

Damn, he's fast!

"No cat's gonna get me, fuck them!" he screamed and proceeded to empty the clip on the drones. One by one I heard them shatter as the lead slammed into them. Then the .45 clicked, letting me know it was empty, I made the choice right there to move as fast as I could around the corner before he could reload.

Before my eyes could even make out the scene in front of me he had already reloaded and was plugging the last of the drones that were scattering in a snake-like pattern. He was too fast in his toxin-induced hyperactivity, and I only made it halfway down the hall when he looked up at me and aimed the gun right at my face. I pulled the blackjack back over my head, trying to build up as much momentum as possible, hoping that in my last few moments the weight of my body would incapacitate him long enough for the others to tackle him. If they were even behind me.

"Hey!" he screamed, more out of recognition than fear. "Hey, Daddy, no. No. I didn't do that. It was Johnny, he broke mom's favorite dishes. Daddy please, not the belt again! I'm sorry! He made me do it!"

I almost broke my stride as I swept up the hallway; did he think I was his father? Why wasn't I an abomination like everyone else? What was different about me? Belt. The blackjack looks like a belt to him. God, was he an abused child?

I stopped dead, crunching the last drone beneath my shoes, and took a deep breath. Noah knelt in the doorframe and threw his arms over his head. "Please Daddy, don't hit me again. I'm sorry. Honest."

I put my arm down but still held the blackjack in my hand. I had no idea what to do, this was a delusional paranoid psychotic with a gun who thinks I am his abusive father. I'm an IT developer, what do I know?

"Noah," I said trying to be as calm as possible. "Noah, do you hear me?"

Noah nodded his head yes; tears ran down his cheeks and over his cradling arms.

"Noah, you have to put the gun down, okay? I don't like you with weapons, you know that, right?"

What else was I gonna do?

He nodded but didn't comply.

"Noah, what did I say?" I reiterated more sternly.

"But they will get me if I do."

Frantically I tried to think of how to walk him out of this situation without abusing him further. As far as he was concerned, I was his father. My own father was a dead-beat drunk who used to beat me too, although I honestly remember fear more than beatings. Fear is a great motivator, and it can do so much, and at that moment I decided not to do what my father would have done, choosing instead the other major influence in my life.

"Son, put the gun down. You know that I am here to protect you, and I won't let anything happen to our family."

"What if they get us? Look what they did to the kittens!"

I shook it off quickly. "Noah, look at me. I'm here now, and I am safe. Put the gun down. I promise we will get out of here and I will take you…" What do non-abusive fathers even do with their kids? "We will get some ice cream and watch some cartoons, okay?"

The gun dropped out of his hand and clanged on the floor. He started sobbing uncontrollably like he'd never really opened up about this before. I ran up, tossing the blackjack down the hall, kicking the gun out of reach, and throwing my arms around him. I had no clue what to do here and approached it the only way I honestly could; two guys with abusive fathers letting it go. Finally.

"It's all right." I hugged him tight, he struggled at first and then relaxed. "It's all right."

With my right hand I reached into my pocket and pulled the antitoxin injector out, ripped the cap off with my teeth, and jabbed it into his shoulder. He hardly flinched.

## Twenty-Seven Year Itch

## Pauline E. Dungate

They say that you are never more than six feet away from a rat. Most of the time that is straight down in the sewers beneath our feet. It's rare to see them, except for that rat that is my brother-in-law. Him, I see far too often but that's one of the problems of working for the same company. He's a supermarket delivery driver while I'm a picker. That is, I make up the on-line orders for him to deliver.

Out the back of the store are a pair of skips. One takes the recyclable rubbish – the cardboard and the plastics. Unsold or spoiled food has its own container with a sealable lid. That's to stop vermin getting in, not to keep the freegans out as some would have you believe. We have strict rules about hygiene, so it was a surprise to see a dead rat (four-legged kind) lying in the middle of the car park. Since I was already wearing plastic gloves, I had no hesitation in picking it up. I was about to chuck it in with the food waste, after all, it's organic and it would go with the rest to the digester when Aaron, the brother-in-law said, "That's the third one this week."

"Have they had pest control in?" I asked. It's always a concern when vermin are found around any place that sells food. If they get inside and start nesting in the storerooms we could get closed down until the place has been decontaminated. Though a few of us might get moved to another store for the duration, which is a pain with the extra travelling, most of the staff would be temporarily laid off with no pay.

"Dunno," Aaron said. "Not here often enough to find out."

That was true. Drivers spend most of their hours on the road delivering the stuff people like me package up for the on-line customers.

I was wondering whether to bother reporting the dead rat when Jane, the supervisor, appeared at the rear door and just stood there. I'm sure she thought I was wasting time gossiping. If it had been anyone but Aaron, that might have been true, but I see enough of him when I'd rather not. Instead, I moved smartly back inside, and gathered the trolley for the next round of picking.

On my break, Jane updated my tablet with the next on-line orders for me to gather. "There's been a run on rolled oats," she said. "You'll have to substitute a branded variety. We are waiting on delivery of fresh goats' milk, so give them the skimmed goat instead if it's not arrived before the orders have to go out."

I nodded. It's always a problem balancing available stock with customer requests, especially when they've booked a specific time slot. There'll be complaints either way – that what they want has been substituted or the order is late. Fortunately, very few customers get totally stroppy. Most of our customers are loyal.

I glanced at the staff room clock. I had another ten minutes before I had to be back in the aisles. Anna from the delicatessen counter plonked herself down in the seat next to mine.

"The squirrels have vanished," she said.

"What squirrels?" I asked. They weren't a creature I had much time for. They might be prettier than rats, but they did steal the bird food I put out on the balcony of my flat. It was supposed to be for the songbirds, not the fluffy grey thieves. I'd watched the pests leap from the lime tree outside my window onto the railing of next door's balcony before scampering along to mine. I kept a water pistol handy to deter them. The fact that I hadn't seen them for a couple of days hadn't registered until Anna mentioned it. I just supposed they were learning to keep out of my sight.

"I walk here over the park," Anna said. "There are always squirrels. Today there are none."

"They'll be back," I said. "They are probably off finding mates."

"You think so?"

"It *is* spring." I drained the rest of my coffee. "Must get back. The orders won't pick themselves."

***

After what Anna had said, I noticed it too. My

flat is on the other side of a park from the bus-stop that I get off at on my way home. There is a children's playground which is largely deserted by the time I get there. Usually there are pigeons strutting around pecking at the crisp fragments dropped by afternoon visitors. Today they were not in evidence. Neither was the blackbird that normally scuttles away from my path. No squirrels.

Later, when I take down my rubbish, there are two dead rats by the bins. Occasionally, well-meaning residents put down poison for them as the council is never bothered by the frequent reports of them. I see Noreen who lives in the bottom corner of the block opposite mine. She is wearing her slippers. She often wanders outside in her slippers, something her daughter frequently chastised her about.

She shuffled in my direction. "Have you seen my cat?" she asked.

I knew the animal. A black and white flat-faced bruiser. I think the breed was described as English. "I'm sorry, Mrs Kaur. I've not seen him."

She frowned, looking a little confused. "He went out last night and didn't come back for his breakfast. Not like him at all."

"I'll let you know if I see him." It never hurts to be nice to neighbours. The cat, an unneutered tom, was probably still out on the razzle. I often heard him yowling outside the flats at night. The uncharitable side of me hoped he'd been selected by the cat-nappers that were rumoured to be stealing pets. Some said it was to make fur coats out of, others that they were being used in nefarious experiments. I didn't believe in either theory.

"Thank you, dear." She wandered off, peering under the bushes that fringed the ground floor of the block.

Usually, I refill my bird feeders when I get in but tonight I didn't need to. During the day there's a regular stream of tits taking the sunflower seeds to secrete them in the nearby trees. They didn't look as if they had been touched. Listening, I couldn't hear any birds either. I'd heard of animals disappearing just before a natural disaster, but this wasn't earthquake country and tornados were extremely rare. Pollution was more likely to be the answer, but the air didn't seem any more toxic than usual. But then, I probably wouldn't know if it was.

I tend to have the door to my balcony open when the weather is warm enough and this spring has been exceptionally warm so far. I face over the park, and towards the main road on the other side so there is always a hum of traffic, even when the trees are in leaf. I'm used to it but this evening as I stood looking out, it seemed very quiet. Almost as if the park was holding its breath. I've always liked that phrase but never knew what it meant before. With dusk, there is usually the rustle of birds and squirrels settling down for the night, the bark of an urban fox or the yowl of cats on the prowl. Tonight, nothing.

That was probably why I heard it. Get outside the town and, in summer, the air is full of the chirrups of crickets. This was a bit like that – a shrill rasping sound. A lost cricket? It came from somewhere out in the park. Then I heard a dog bark, followed by a shriek. There was a laugh. Someone was taking their pet for an evening walk. Likely they had disturbed an insect. I closed my door, pulled the curtains and forgot about it.

***

"Any more dead rats?" Aaron said next morning as we let ourselves into the staff entrance of the supermarket. I always tried to arrive before he did, but it didn't always work. Our shifts were scheduled for the same start time.

"Actually, yes," I said. "There were two by the bins at the flat."

He told me that Lonnie (that's my sister) had seen one on the canal towpath on her way home. "And I saw one in the garden," he said. He then went on to give me a graphic description of it. He does it because he knows I'm not squeamish and he's trying to get a rise out of me. Fortunately, I don't have to spend much time with him and I grabbed the tablet with the orders on it and headed into the store to start picking.

The morning was relatively peaceful, unless you count the toddler that ran up and down the aisles screaming with delight. If kids aren't causing real mayhem or getting in the way of more elderly customers, the management is reasonably tolerant. Better to have a happy child than one lying on the floor having a tantrum because Mum won't let him open the sweets until they've been paid for.

The scream that signalled trouble was the shriek similar to the one I'd heard the previous evening. As it didn't sound human, I didn't rush to find out – let someone closer deal with it. Karen, who was stacking the shelves nearby, glanced in my direction.

"Not heard one of them since last I was in Jamaica," she said.

"What is it?" I asked.

"We call them cicada. Didn't think you had them here."

"Sounded like a weird grasshopper."

"Maybe." Karen went back to her job; I went back to mine.

When I took my afternoon break, there was a notice pinned to the staff notice-board. It told us that strange insects had been seen in the car park. They were not cockroaches. That was good to know. If roaches were found in the store, we might have to close until management was satisfied they'd been dealt with. Even if they had been, we'd have deny it to customers.

I saw my first one that evening. It was sitting on the railing of the balcony. It was about an inch and a half long and very pretty. Its eyes were bright red and the transparent wings veined with yellow. As I went to get a closer look, it took off with a shriek. Definitely what I had heard the night before. There must have been more around as the leaves of the nearest tree rustled and there was the kind of hissing you get with crickets. I closed my door firmly.

However attractive the insect was, I didn't want it and its mates inside with me.

I don't watch much TV. I confess I'm more into gaming than soaps, but I do like to have the radio on. I keep it tuned to a local station that punctuates the music with half-hourly news shots. What caught my ear was a plea to keep pets indoors as some were disappearing and being found dead. I thought about Noreen's cat and wondered if it had been unlucky. There was no reason given for the animals dying. Perhaps it was too soon and they had to do tests. My sister has a Westie. A white one that always looks grubby even just after a bath. She let it out in the garden to do its business but otherwise it never went out without her. The garden was very secure. I was very surprised to get a call from her later in the evening.

Lonnie is easy to upset. Aaron does it all the time, one of his rat-like characteristics. When she called, she was hysterical and it took a while to get sense out of her. At first, I thought she was talking about Aaron when she said he was dead. I finally twigged that she was talking about the dog. She'd let him out for his evening pootle in the garden. When he didn't come back in, she gone looking for him with a flashlight. She found him in the middle of the lawn.

"There were these insects all over him," she said. "They were hissing at me."

"Are you sure he was dead?"

"He wasn't moving. What am I going to do?"

"Where's Aaron?" I asked. *He should be dealing*

*with this*, I thought, *not me.*

"He went to the pub. His phone's off."

He might have gone to the pub but I doubted he was still there. Not that I'd say anything to Lonnie. "Do you want me to come round?" I asked, hoping she'd say no, expecting otherwise.

"Would you? Please?"

"It'll take me half an hour, at least."

"Please."

Grumbling to myself, mostly about Aaron and his inability to be around when Lonnie needed him, I stuffed my arms into my jacket and grabbed my bag before dishing out over the park to the bus-stop. It was only as I reached the other side that I became aware of the chittering hiss that was coming from all around, not just in the canopy of the trees. I didn't stop to consider it as a bus pulled in and I just caught it before the doors slammed shut. Something flew in past me as I scrambled for a seat. One of the cicada things zoomed around me before landing on the back of the seat in front. Annoyed, I flicked it off.

Lonnie's house is in the middle of a terraced row, the kind with minimal front gardens but long narrow ones at the back. A fairly standard house in a town that had sprung up on a green field site only a quarter of a century ago. I'd hardly rung the bell, when the door was jerked open and my sister launched herself into my arms, sobbing.

I peeled her off me long enough to get inside and shuck off my coat.

"Have you made tea?" I asked. A brew is our

mum's answer to most problems and Lonnie is much the same. When she shook her head, I stepped down into the kitchen and put the kettle on. If the dog was already dead, I didn't see much point in rushing out to examine the corpse. Calming Lonnie down was much more important. And mentally cursing Aaron for making himself unavailable.

Two mugs later and listening to Lonnie telling me how much she loved the Westie over and over, I decided I would have to deal with the body. I didn't particularly want to go digging holes in the garden after dark – I'd leave that for Aaron – but I could move it from the patch of lawn so Lonnie would not have to see it in the morning when she looked out of the window. I'm familiar with the place – I'm usually round alternate weeks – so finding the rubbish bags was easy.

Lonnie kept a flashlight on the windowsill beside the back door in case she had to go out to the bins by the back gate, or to find the dog. I opened the door and ducked as one of those cicada things buzzed past me. As the lesser problem, I decided to deal with it later.

With the light in one hand and the plastic bag in the other, I stepped onto the patio and pulled the door closed behind me. Insects flashed through the beam. Not moths, I thought it too early in the year and the numbers had dropped in recent years. More cicadas?

I noticed the high-pitched hum that had nothing to do with traffic or overhead wires but was more concerned with finding the dog. I cast the beam over the back garden. To start with I saw nothing, then at the periphery of the light was a movement. In the flower bed rather than on the grass. I directed the light in that direction. For a moment I thought the dog was still alive – it was twitching. It was old and could easily have keeled over naturally. Then I saw the insects. Their wings shimmered in the beam and they were swarming over it. Tufts of off-white fur showed red between their bodies. I remembered what Aaron had told me that morning about the rat he'd found. It looked as if it had been chewed by another rodent. Maybe they had already got at the dog and the cicadas had been drawn to the smell. I had no idea what the insects ate. Since they sounded like grasshoppers and were in the trees, I'd assumed they were a bit like locusts and half-expected the trees to be stripped on leaves come morning.

I wasn't about to leave my sister's pet in the dirt. I dashed towards it, waving the torch around and yelling at the insects. They arose in a shrieking cloud. I shook my head, partially deafened. I dropped the torch, grabbed the dog and stuffed it in the plastic bag. It was undignified but better than leaving it there. Retrieving the torch, I hefted it down the garden and dumped it in the bin. Then I realised I was crying.

I hadn't particularly liked the animal, but it was my sister's pet. She'd had it twelve years, longer than she'd been married. Lonnie was already upset. My treatment of her dog would make her grief worse, but I wasn't going to leave it for vermin.

As I returned to the kitchen, I found that my

hands were itching. In the light there, I found them covered with tiny cuts. They were bleeding more than I would have expected and the skin around them was numb. I also felt giddy. That I put down to the trauma of dealing with the crisis in the garden and Lonnie's ongoing grief. Sitting down seemed like a good idea. Instead, I propped myself up by the sink, scrubbed my hands and smeared antiseptic cream on the cuts.

I was ready to stagger into the sitting room to rejoin Lonnie when there was a scream. Two, actually. One was Lonnie. The other I'd come to recognise as the cicada's warning shriek. I lurched rather than ran to the living room. One of the insects was batting itself against the window.

"It bit me," Lonnie said.

"Show me."

She held out her bloodied hand showing the small Y-shaped cut like the ones on my own hands. She started to scratch at the skin around it. I picked up one of Lonnie's magazines, rolled it and lashed out with it at the hissing insect. It fell to the floor and I stamped on it. It gave a satisfying crunch.

"I feel funny," Lonnie said.

"So do I." I sat down next to her and put my arm around her shoulders. I closed my eyes as the room spun as if I'd overdone the gin.

Next thing I knew was Aaron shaking me. "What you doing here?" That's what I think he said. My mind was fuzzy.

"Couldn't get you. Phone off," I mumbled. Lonnie's head lolled against my shoulder. I tried again. "Dog's dead."

"You shitting me?"

"Nope. Body's in the bin. You bury it." I pushed Lonnie gently off my shoulder and stood up. I felt a little wobbly.

"You leaving?" he asked.

"I got a home to go to." I didn't much fancy the walk back across town. There'd be no more buses until morning now. Neither did I want to hang around here.

"There's lots of big insects flying around out there." I wasn't sure if he said it out of concern or trying to worry me.

"Yeah. They bite, too." A couple of things suddenly came together. "I think they have anaesthetic in their saliva. Like mosquitos or horseflies."

"Where did you get that from? Your games?"

That sounded more like the Aaron I knew. "You'd be surprised what you can learn from gaming. Got any insect repellent left from last summer?" He and Lonnie tend to head for Spain each year and my sister is sensitive to insect bites.

"Probably. Why?"

"So I can get home. Unless you want me kipping on your sofa."

"I'll find it."

I helped myself to the can of fly killer I'd seen in the same cupboard as the bin bags. I sprayed face, hands and coat with the repellent Aaron found and headed out. There were a lot of the insects clustering around the streetlamp and crawling on the grass. Less on the road itself, where there were signs of crushed carcasses. I was twitchy all the way. I kept to the roads, taking the long way round rather than cutting across the park, and managed to get home without being bitten again. I refused to think about what would happen if I fell asleep under a tree.

Once inside I checked myself over carefully. I didn't want anything clinging to my clothes, then went round the flat making sure all doors and windows were secure, spraying fly killer along all the cracks.

***

I contemplated calling in sick the next day but, in the end, headed out, sticking to the roads. A glance out of the windows had showed me thousands of the creatures. They clung to the trunks of the trees coating them in a thick, moving mass. Those on the ground climbed over them to get higher. They weren't flying but they were singing. The sound, someone described it as being like tinnitus, followed me all the way, getting louder when I got closer to the trees. Occasionally, one would take off shrieking. They didn't seem as active as at night. People were trying to avoid them, causing havoc when they strayed into the road.

At the store, Jane corralled us all into the staff room. Aaron, I noticed, wasn't there. I had to assume he was staying off to cope with Lonnie's crisis. I'd text later.

When she thought she had everyone, Jane started by stating the obvious. "You'll all have noticed the insects outside. Head office says we should open as usual."

"Are they dangerous?" Anna asked.

"They bite," I said.

Jane glared at me. "Don't be a scaremonger. They are big grasshoppers."

"Look more like cockroaches," someone at the back of the room said.

"Those are not dangerous either," Jane said. "Just unhygienic. Needless, we don't want them inside. Get rid of them discretely. Customers mustn't be alarmed."

"Will we get customers?" Karen asked. "We should go home 'til the outbreak is over."

"The store stays open," Jane said firmly.

Brian, one of the stockmen, said, "We should never have built here. Grandpa said it was a mistake. No-one listened."

Jane ignored him. "Right. To work everyone. We have jobs to do."

I was curious about what Brian had said, so I kept my eyes open to get a chance to talk to him. None of us who lived or worked in the town had been here twenty-five years ago. This was a new town, built on fields which, it was claimed, had no agricultural value, to offset the ever-increasing need for homes. The place was older than me, just, so I'd never known a world without it.

When I'd done the first batch of picking, I trundled it out back ready for scheduling and loading into the delivery vans. Normally, the service doors are left open. I spotted Brian manoeuvring a load from a delivery lorry with his forklift. The moment he cleared the gate, he slammed the door and stamped on the insects that had crawled in while it was open. I went over before he had a chance to head off into the storeroom's depths.

"What did you mean when you said we shouldn't have built there?"

"It's what my Grandpa says. He gets a bit forgetful at times, but he's been saying the crawlers are coming back."

"What are the crawlers?"

"Not sure. It could be these insect things. He says they always come back."

"It's not the first time then?"

"He says last time they came was when my brother was born."

"When was that?"

"He's twenty-seven this year."

"Does your Grandpa say what happened when they came?"

"I'm not sure I believe him, but he says they ate the cows." Brian gave me a wry smile. "Gotta get on."

The conversation left me frustrated. There was so much more I wanted to know. I'd seen what the crawlers appeared to be doing to Lonnie's dog; I'd felt the effects of the bites. I scratched at my hands. The skin around the bites itched, like the aftermath of a mosquito bite but more intense. I was suddenly nervous. No, I'm not squeamish, but I was scared. If they could eat a cow, they could eat me. The thought worried me through the rest of the morning. I made mistakes. I didn't know how long the crawlers would be around.

As the afternoon ran down and the sky started to pale, I couldn't stand the attempts at normality. It wasn't my shift end, but I grabbed my coat, lifted two cans of fly killer and left. I'd face the consequences later. All I wanted was to be safe in my flat.

The automatic doors of the store opened, letting out a blast of warm air. They were there, a shifting mass in the car park. They were moving towards the doors, the few cars parked up. It was the warmth that attracted them. Only a few were flying. They crunched beneath my feet. I saw a couple of schoolkids. They were kicking the crawlers. I wanted to shout at them to stop, that they were in danger. Maybe I should have. I knew they'd laugh at me so I hurried, the fly spray can poised in my hand like the pepper spray Lonnie always held before her when she went out alone at night.

The park was heaving with them when I skirted it. As the light faded, more were taking to the air. I saw heaps of them. I saw the shape of someone waiting at the bus-stop. They were waving their hands around as crawlers flew towards them. I saw them stumble and fall, and the insects mound up over them. I ran.

The creatures were piled at the door to the flats. I sprayed them, keeping my finger on the trigger long after they'd cleared from my path. I fumbled the key – I didn't dare take my gloves off. If I exposed my skin, they would bite me. I wrenched the door open and got inside, slamming it behind me. Some tumbled in after me. Others flew at the wood. I heard the thumps of them hitting it even above the continual sound – a hissing punctuated by screams. I stomped and sprayed the ones that had got in before fleeing up the stairs to my flat.

My heart was racing as I thudded my door closed, heard the snick of the lock catch. But I didn't feel safe. I could still hear them and I had to search the flat, reassure myself that there were none inside, that they couldn't get in. I sprayed the windows and door until the can was empty. Then I turned all the lights on. I had an idea that they preferred it dark and I wanted to see then if they forced their way in. Could enough of them break the window? Could they chew through the woodwork? I felt besieged.

I wrapped myself up to expose as little skin as possible. I didn't care if I was too hot. I just didn't want to be eaten. I wasn't intending to sleep, I wanted to keep watch. Coffee worked for a while but then it was morning and my phone was ringing. It was Lonnie.

"Are you all right?" she said.

"Yeah. You?"

"Guess so. I was worried. There… there's dead insects all over the place. Aaron's sweeping them off the patio. He… he wanted to come over last night. See you were all right. You weren't answering your phone. I wouldn't let him."

"I didn't hear it," I said. "The crawlers were making too much noise. Tell Aaron I'll see him at work."

I went to the window and pulled back the curtains. The balcony was covered with dead insects. They were beginning to smell musty. I fetched a broom and began to sweep them over the drop, hearing the rustle of friable wings. A sparrow hopped onto the railing and chirruped at me. It was a beautiful sound. I started to cry. Aaron had been concerned about me. He might be a rat, but I'd rather a live rat than a million deadly cockroaches.

## Patient One

## John Ryland

Doctor Steven Bilkens looked up from the file on his desk and shook his head. He rubbed his eyes with his fingertips and breathed a worried sigh. Pulling open the top left drawer in his desk, he produced a bottle of eyedrops and applied them to each eye. The late nights were catching up with him.

In his thirty years as a biologist, he'd seen a great many strange and wonderful things. In the last twelve as head of the Research Institute of Molecular Life, the things he saw were more strange than wonderful. The world was changing. Germs evolved and grew in ways no one could predict, yet through every pandemic, humans adapted. From the beginning of time, the Earth has resisted mankind's presence. Every novel pathogen had been overcome. From the Bubonic Plague to Sars, humans survived. The report before him, however, was unlike anything he'd ever seen. It read like a cheap science fiction novel, but unfortunately, it wasn't. In it, he heard the whispers of the first bell tolls for humanity. If it turned out to be true, it wasn't the beginning of the end, but the beginning of the beginning of the end.

They were calling it Depersonalization Disorder with Dominant Trait Hypersensitivity, but the name fell well short of what he'd read in the report. There were six subjects downstairs, locked in isolation rooms, but rumors of more surfaced every day. They were limited to six because there were no more rooms. That was more than enough to know things were going to be bad.

Standing, he closed the report that had taken him an hour to read and carried it to the shredder. He slid it in, watching until the manila file folder and its contents were reduced to pulp. Like every other report on this sickness, the Institute was making sure there wasn't a paper trail. If word got out to the public, there'd be a panic. Keeping his team calm was hard enough.

His eyes darted to the clear receptacle beneath the shredder, now mostly full. He'd read a lot about this disorder, now it was time to see it for himself. He didn't relish the idea of going downstairs but couldn't put it off any longer.

***

The air pumped into the isolation suit was dry and smelled of chemicals. It wasn't pleasant, but it was reassuring. Better than taking a chance on contracting whatever the subjects had. Months of tests still hadn't fully revealed the transmission capabilities. There were six here, collected from across the country, surely all six hadn't developed the same symptoms independently. Of course, it was possible but highly unlikely. All six had gotten it somehow. The question was how.

Steven Bilkens turned to his left and nodded to the man next to him wearing a matching white encapsulation suit. Charles Harless worked in the isolation department, monitoring the subjects. A shudder ran through him at the thought. Truth be known, he didn't feel safe being in the same building with them. Every night after he went home, he had to fight the urge to collect his wife and fly to an island somewhere and spend the remaining time he had left drinking rum and making love on the beach. Of course, he'd never done either, but he wanted to.

"Ready?" Charles asked, in a deep voice that would have been comforting had they been anywhere else.

Steven offered a thumbs up and Charles reached out, holding a key card in his gloved hand.

Steven stepped over the threshold and waited while Charles closed the doors behind them. The sound of his heart thundered in his ears inside the suit, his breaths coming in nervous pants. Every exhale created a tiny patch of fog on the face shield. He could already feel himself beginning to sweat. He hated coming down here and only did it when necessary. His lofty perch in the Director's office suited him better.

When Charles walked past, motioning him to follow, Steven reminded himself that they'd housed every major transmittable disease known to man without incident. It helped until his mind reminded him that they'd also never dealt with something like this. There was so much about the disorder that they didn't know.

The first room they came to was on the right. The front wall was two-inch-thick polymer glass, giving them an unobstructed view of the patient. The speaker in his suit crackled and Doctor Harless' voice filled his helmet again.

"They can't see us. It's basically like the glass in a police interrogation room." He nodded, his movements exaggerated in the bulky suit. "But a lot thicker."

Steven nodded back, then turned his attention to the glass. The man inside the ten-by-ten room was crouched in the far corner, barely visible in the shadows. When the lights came up, operated by the tablet in Doctor Harless' hands, the patient looked around.

Steven looked into the sunken eyes of the patient and saw only fear and anxiety. The man, clothed only in a plain white hospital gown, looked scared to death. The speaker in his suit crackled again and he was informed that Patient Three had a dominant trait of passivity. The decision to not use their real names had come down from the top brass. They'd said it was to spare the patients' families in the case of an information leak, but Steven knew better. These patients would all die here. Not having names would make euthanizing them easier if things came to that.

Steven nodded, remembering the report. The

man had been a high school librarian. The word that his friends and co-workers used most often to describe him was "nervous". He was a nice guy, humble, passive, but had managed his anxiety enough to forge a career and buy a small house just outside Columbia, South Carolina. Then everything changed.

The Depersonalization Disorder had stripped him of everything except for his dominant trait which, unfortunately for him, was anxiousness. There was no self-awareness, no emotions, no personalization of the human form. He was blank, except for his anxiety. Like the other patients, the lack of empathy made him dangerous. As hard as it was to believe now, the meek man huddled in the corner had stabbed two teenage students, killing one of them. All they'd done to draw his ire was to knock on the door to his office. He'd calmly gotten up, answered the door, and stabbed each of them in the right eye with a number 2 pencil. When the cops got there, they found him hiding beneath his desk mumbling about how the boys were "out to get him".

"It's astounding when you think about it."

Steven looked at his co-worker and nodded. He'd been reading extensively about personality disorders, and dissociative disorders, but they all paled compared to this. There always remained at least a scrap of the person they used to be, some subconscious tag that kept them grounded in who they were. That was not the case with this thing. This was completely different.

"Aside from their hypersensitive dominant trait,

there isn't a shred of humanity left in them."

"And the remedies haven't affected that at all?"

Steven watched the other doctor shake his head and then turned back to the room. The man had crawled beneath the small cot mounted on the wall. Curled in a ball with his hands over his head, he looked more like a dog that had been beaten regularly than a grown man.

Steven's eyes diverted to the glass, and he watched the reflection of Doctor Harless pass behind him. In the white isolation suit, his translucent reflection looked like a ghost. His eyes went back to the man cowering beneath the cot and shook his head. That's all he was, a ghost of his former self, void of everything that made him human. A word tickled the back of his mind, but he pushed it aside. It was a fitting word for the condition, but he refused to use it. It was too cliched. Besides, his bosses had sent out a memo forbidding the use of the "Z-word". Words like that scared people. Even trained scientists.

Sighing, he moved along, joining Doctor Harless in front of the next room. Steven gasped as his eyes roved over the blood-smeared walls. Lines of blood, in groups of four, marred every wall, including the inside of the glass before him. Doctor Harless gave him a nod, then brought the lights up.

Steven recoiled visibly. The woman slept sprawled on the cot, her back against the wall. The bloody front of her gown was hiked up to her waist, revealing her groin, swollen almost beyond recognition. One hand, bloody to the wrist, lay across her thigh while the other clutched her privates, thankfully hiding them from view. The immediate area around her crotch was a sea of deep purple bruises, smeared with blood.

"Are we treating her for pain? Infection?"

Doctor Harless nodded. "Antibiotics above the regular treatments, but I don't think it matters."

"How so?"

"None of the patients have had so much as a hint of an infection. We take blood tests every week and do a full workup. Whatever causes this disorder also seems to prevent traditional infection rates."

Steven nodded, recalling the report he'd read on Patient Six. The woman, in her 40s, had been diagnosed with breast cancer two years ago. Every test they'd run on her so far had revealed no sign of cancer. Some of the other doctors upstairs were excited about this fact. Steven wasn't. To him, it was like killing a spider with a nuclear bomb.

"What about pain?" he asked, grimacing as he scrutinized the battered pelvic region of the woman. "That's got to hurt."

Doctor Harless shook his head. "As far as we can tell, they feel no pain either."

Steven sighed, bringing his hand up to rub his face, but found only the plastic face shield in the suit helmet. He shook his head and nodded for the doctor to turn the lights back down. The last thing he wanted to happen was for the woman to wake up and start forcefully violating herself again.

"Have we tried restraints on her?' he asked as they moved to the next room.

"Yes, but she chews through them."

"Even the leather?" Steven asked.

Doctor Harless nodded. "It just takes a little longer." He stopped, turning to Steven. "The reports are very thorough. You have been reading them?"

Steven nodded. He had read every one of them multiple times. He'd read Charles' reports, the reports from the pathologists, the pharmacists, the microbiologists, and every other report available. He knew about the restraints but needed to feel like he was contributing. So far, nothing anyone upstairs had done had affected the patients at all. No medicines or combinations of medicines had as much as dented the effects of the disorder. They hadn't even isolated the pathogen that caused it and he was beginning to wonder if there was one. None of the patients here were related or even lived near the others. They came from all walks of life. There was a librarian from Arkansas. The woman they'd just seen was a stay-at-home mother with six kids from Arizona. There was a construction worker from Chicago, an artist, and a banker. As far as they could tell, none of them had crossed paths. Each was completely independent of the other, yet they shared the same depersonalization disorder, highlighted by their own unique dominant trait hypersensitivity.

"This is a bad one. Patient One," Doctor Harless said, drawing Steven from his thoughts. "You ready?"

Steven nodded that he was ready though he knew he wasn't. Patient One was the banker. His dominant trait was aggression. The reports on him read like horror stories. He was also resistant to the sedation, making the situation exponentially more difficult.

The room was pitch black, but as the lights came up slowly, a shape emerged. Patient One stood in the center of the room, motionless. His dark, blank eyes stared straight at them. He was completely naked, his six-foot frame dripping with sweat. The metal bands affixed around his wrists had rubbed bloody rings above and below them, due largely to his struggling against the steel cables that tethered him to the floor. His ankles were in almost as bad shape as his wrists.

The muscles in his arms flexed as he raised his clenched fists, pulling against the restraints. His biceps bulged as the cables grew taut, but he applied more pressure to them. His body began to shake as he strained, pulling on the cables until, finally, he relaxed and lowered his fists to his sides. He paused, his gaze fixed on them, then began the process again.

"All day, every day," Doctor Harless said. "That's all he does. It's like a workout. He's gotten stronger since he's been here."

"Are we confident in the restraints?" Steven asked, his voice anything but.

"You could tow your car with those cables, Doctor."

Steven's eyes washed over the muscular frame of the patient, then went to the cable attached to the patient's right wrist. The man raised his arm, pulling against the cable. It stretched tight but held. He made a mental note to recheck the tensile strength of the cables and a thought ran through his mind, sending a shudder through him. If this man got free, he'd probably kill every one of them with his bare hands. The guards would have to shoot him. Probably multiple times.

He closed his eyes and drew in a calming breath, but a more terrifying thought occurred to him. There may be more like him out there somewhere, potentially hundreds, maybe thousands. Void of humanity, of compassion, and driven by an all-consuming rage. There would be no stopping them. These ones, he thought, would be at the top of the food chain.

Patient One had come to them from somewhere in Kansas. They'd transported him in an armored car like the ones they carried money in. He was wearing two sets of shackles on his hands and two on his feet. They strapped a hockey mask on him after he'd bitten a large chunk out of an officer's cheek.

He'd been here the longest and, like the others, hadn't spoken a word. All the patients were nonverbal, and none showed a desire to eat or drink. The MDs said their bodies were living off fat stores. Patient One certainly looked like it. There wasn't an ounce of fat on the man.

As the doctors watched, the man squatted and defecated on the floor. When he was done, he stood and went back to his routine, pulling against the cables.

"Okay," Steven said, letting Doctor Harless know that he'd seen enough. The lights lowered in the room again, but something told him the man was still there, doing the same thing. Like all the other patients, his dominant trait was the only outward display he exhibited. They'd react that way until their body either passed out from exhaustion, or they were drugged to unconsciousness to allow for tests and cleaning. Like robots, programmed for one purpose, it was what they did. All day, every day, like the doctor said.

"We call this next one 'The Professor', mostly because he was, well, a professor." Doctor Harless' chuckle sounded hollow in his suit. When Steven didn't laugh with him, his smile vanished, and he slowly brought the lights up in the room before them.

Steven nodded. Patient Two was a mathematics professor at some prestigious college in New England. He couldn't recall which one but remembered being impressed when he'd read his bio. He watched as the lights came up on the small man in the room before him. Not only was the patient short, around five foot six, but he was also petite. His gray hair was a mess atop his head, not dissimilar to pictures he'd seen of Albert Einstein. Of course, this only fed into the persona.

The man was staring at the wall to his left, but when the lights brightened, he looked at the glass. His deep-set eyes seemed fixed on the two doctors outside. His head tilted to the side slightly and his brow furrowed.

"What's he doing?" Steven asked.

Doctor Harless shrugged. "Thinking, I guess. That's all he does."

Steven stared back at the man. "What do you figure he's thinking about?"

"A way to get out, if I had to guess."

Steven's head snapped around. "You think so?"

"I'd say so. For days after he got here, he just examined the room. Measuring and remeasuring. He's touched and examined every square inch. He's figured out that this front wall is smooth. Probably deduced that it was glass while the others are solid concrete. He usually comes to the glass and stares at us."

"But he can't see us."

"No, but he's a genius. Glass wall, lights go up. He's undoubtedly extrapolated that he's being observed."

"That's a departure from the others."

Doctor Harless nodded. "Yes, but his dominant trait is his intellect. He's a thinker, unlike our other friends."

"There's no way to actually do it, is there?" Steven asked. "Get out, I mean."

Doctor Harless shook his head. "The door is flush to the wall and hermetically sealed. It's only opened by mechanisms on the outside which are controlled in a locked room outside of this wing. There are redundancies built into the system. It takes two people acting in concert to open each door." He saw the unease in Steven's face and smiled. "But even if he did, the wing itself is sealed as well."

"Yes. Good."

"Besides, he's nonviolent."

"I wouldn't be so sure." Steven watched the patient shuffle to the glass. He stood with his hands clasped behind his back, staring at them. His eyes moved slowly beneath his bushy, unkept eyebrows. "We don't know everything there is to know about this disorder."

"True." Doctor Harless watched the patient as he turned from the glass and began pacing the floor.

"What's he doing now?" Steven asked.

"Counting how long the lights stay on." When Steven gave him a curious glance, he added, "As best we can tell. But I must admit, I don't know why."

"He's a mathematician," Steven said approaching the glass. "He's looking for patterns." Turning back to Doctor Harless he added, "Redundancies."

"Doctor Bilkens, this facility was built to prevent pathogens from escaping. Each of these rooms is sealed to that end. If a germ cannot escape one of them, I assure you that a patient can't."

Steven nodded. "Let's hope those aren't humanity's famous last words."

"I assure you it's nothing like that, Doctor. And quite frankly, I'm a little surprised someone in your position would say something like that."

In the helmet, Steven's sigh sounded tired, worried. "Look…"

"Doctor Bilkens, I can personally assure you that

this facility is secure. As I said…" The doctor stopped suddenly, interrupted by another voice coming over his intercom. "Yes, Ms. Boatwright?" he asked, responding to the technician they'd spoken to on the way in.

"I'm sorry to bother you, but Doctor Bilkens is being called to the conference room. They said it was important."

"What for?" Steven asked, having heard the same message. He'd sat in on countless sessions, hashing out possible treatments and causes for the disorder. All of them had been "important" yet none had yielded any results. He wasn't looking forward to another.

"I'm not sure, Doctor, they didn't say."

Steven sighed and tossed his hands into the air. "I must go through decom. It'll be a minute."

"Yessir."

Doctor Harless shrugged as they started back toward the door. "At least you were spared the worst of things."

"It gets worse?" Steven asked.

Doctor Harless nodded. "Much."

***

Steven Bilkens smoothed his tie as he took his seat at the head of the expansive mahogany table. Half a dozen faces stared back at him. When he'd assembled them, he felt sure that some of the greatest minds in their respective fields would figure this thing out in a month. Even though no resources were spared, they'd produced very little. In many ways, they were as lost on this thing as they'd been at the start.

"My apologies, ladies and gentlemen, I was downstairs. One can't rush through the decontamination chamber." A tense chuckle spread through the people sitting at the table, most of whom were younger than he. Everyone was staring at him, except one painfully thin red-haired woman typing on her laptop. She wasn't his favorite team member and not bothering to look up was disrespectful, but she was a good researcher. "Shall we start?"

"Uh, yes sir. We think we've found a commonality."

Steven looked at the young man with wire-rimmed glasses, watching him shrink beneath his gaze. "Go on."

"Hot springs," the man said.

"Hot Springs. Like the city in Arkansas, or the geothermal pools."

The young woman next to him cleared her throat and slid closer to the table. "Maybe both, sir. Every patient downstairs may have visited a hot spring in the last six months."

"May have?" Steven asked. "Either they did or didn't."

Halfway down the table, an older man sighed. He wasn't quite Steven's age, but he was older than the others. "Sir, four of the six patients did visit a natural hot spring within the last six months. One visited Yellowstone National." He shrugged. "We placed the first three right off. It took some digging to find about the fourth."

"So, the commonality is natural spring water?"

"More precisely, geothermally heated water. The patient who visited Yellowstone went to see Old Faithful."

"Okay." Steven clasped his hands before him. "Myself not being a geologist, fill me in on things. I'm presuming that they didn't visit the same hot spring."

"Correct, sir. I'm no geologist either, but from what I understand, all these hot springs, geothermal pools, and geysers all derive their water from the same deep-earth pools."

Steven's eyes narrowed as his mind went to work. "What are we thinking? Heavy metals? A toxin?"

"We still don't have that answer, sir."

"We've done countless toxicity tests. Nothing is out of the ordinary with any patient, except the woman from Arizona having high levels of tch in her system when they brought her in."

"True, but could we have missed something?" The younger members of the crowd looked astonished at the suggestion.

"Doubtful." Steven shook his head. "People have been going to these things for hundreds of years, thousands probably. They're thought to be healthy. They test the waters, don't they? Why would it start now?"

"Well, sir, here's the thing. If you'll bear with me. My daughter is a geologist, well, she's in school to become one. When we discovered the commonality of the first three, I remembered something she was talking about while she was home for Christmas break. She was going on and on about a deep-focus earthquake. At the time I didn't think much about it because it didn't make the news." The man waved his hand. "You can't feel them. Anyway, one occurred at an extreme depth. In the lower mantle."

"What does that have to do with our patients?"

"It is possible that such a deep earthquake could change something, release a chemical into the water supply that feeds these things. These geothermal pools."

Steven sighed, bringing his clasped fists to his mouth. It sounded plausible, and it was the best lead they'd had so far. "When did this earthquake happen?"

"Eight months ago."

"We've been working on the assumption that it would take months for a pathogen to have such a profound effect on the brain. That makes the timing critical. We'll need all you can find on this earthquake."

"Yes sir," the man said, opening the laptop before him.

"Sir?" A man on the right raised his hand. Steven recognized him as one of the neurologists but couldn't recall his name. "If I may. The effect would depend on the level of exposure and the strength of the pathogen, for lack of a better word. If something new were released and the patients were exposed to a novel substance, there's literally no telling how quickly it could affect the human brain."

Steven shook his head and turned to the young man who'd started the conversation. "We must look at this objectively. First, we don't know if it's even accurate, or if it affects everyone the same way. There is a multitude of variables." He sighed. "I mean, we don't even know how many vents were affected, if any, or how many people were exposed."

The woman behind the laptop spoke up. "In 2018 7.9 million people visited hot springs in the United States. Plus 4.8 million visitors to Yellowstone, where they presumably went to see Old Faithful." She scanned the faces looking at her before adding, "It's their biggest attraction."

"So that's roughly twelve million people. Halve that to only include those within the last six months and you get six million people." A gasp went up from the table as everyone imagined an extra million people for each patient downstairs.

"Actually, Doctor, adjusting for peak visitation months and general trends, the number is probably closer to eight million." She hesitated then added, "Sir."

Steven sat back in his chair with a sigh. "I want these geologists who discovered this earthquake here asap. Also, get field teams assembled and get them to every damned pool of hot water we can find. We need samples and extensive testing. We're going to have to get some evidence before this notion goes any further."

"Sir, shouldn't we say something?"

Steven shook his head. "What would we say? Are you suggesting we go on the evening news with suspicions and innuendo? Tell them about Johnson's daughter's…"

"Jorgenson," the man corrected. "Sir."

"Yes. Yes. Jorgenson. We tell them about this deep earthquake and that potentially millions of people may have been exposed to something that we can't even identify? Very few people even know these patients exist, that this situation exists. It would start a panic."

"I know, but if people are turning into z…"

Steven Bilkens held up his hand, stopping the word in the young scientist's throat. "Don't even say it."

"Sir?"

Steven's eyes went to the woman with the laptop. "Don't say it."

"No, sir. There's something else."

He sighed. "What?"

"It seems there are also several lines of organic beauty and hygiene products that contain water from hot springs."

"Of course there are," he moaned. "Numbers?"

"I don't have product numbers yet, sir, but combined sales exceed twenty million dollars in the last six months. There's everything from mud masks to eye drops."

"Eye drops?" Steven asked.

She shrugged. "Who knew?"

"That may explain the other two patients who hadn't visited a geothermal vent," Jorgenson added.

Steven pushed back from the table and stood with a grunt. "Let's go back over every test. Look for anything anomalous, no matter how minor. Let's see if we can isolate this thing. And get those damned geologists over here. I want to know what the hell is down there that could cause this." He rubbed his eyes with both hands and sighed again. "I've got to take this to my bosses and watch them go berserk. Time is of the essence, people, but be thorough. If something is there, we have to find it."

***

The desk chair groaned loudly in the darkness as Steven Bilkens leaned back. Stretching through a yawn, he checked his watch, discovering that it was three in the morning. He should have gone home ten hours ago but knew it would have been useless. He wouldn't be able to sleep anyway. The enormity of the situation, the sheer numbers involved, would keep him awake.

He looked at his notes, hastily jotted down during a teleconference with one of the geologists who's discovered the quake. The words mid-mantle, inert substance, and fissure meant less to him now than when he'd written them. "Unknown materials" was beneath them, underlined with two heavy strokes. "Localized?" was next to it. Besides that, he'd written "North America". He sighed again. The best-case scenario was that it was localized, but even that would affect all of North America.

"Deep ocean vents" was next, but the words that kept him in his chair were "Probable global occurrence". The man had talked for another ten minutes, but Steven scarcely remembered a word he said. The possibility was far from conclusive, but with each passing hour, his gut told him they were either right or at least on the right trail.

He sighed, shaking his head at the whole situation. He'd seen the movies, watched while rotting zombies ate people's faces off. All that was science fiction, but this was real. The six people downstairs weren't the undead, but they weren't alive either. At least not as the same people they used to be. He'd scoffed at every movie, citing the impossibility of a zombie horde, but now that he was faced with the possibility, it didn't seem so funny.

His thoughts drifted to Patient One. In his mind, he saw the man's muscles bulging as he pulled against the steel cables, relentless in his efforts. If he had to go one-on-one with that man, he wouldn't last two seconds, and neither would anyone he knew. He'd be ripped apart and discarded like a paper bag. The thought that there could be thousands just like him was unfathomable.

Steven looked at the numbers on the screen before him, trying to focus his tired eyes. The years of staring at a computer screen and reading files were catching up with him. Extending a hand, he opened his top left desk drawer. Digging through the assorted junk, he found a bottle of eye drops.

"Pure Tears," he said, reading the bottle as he unscrewed the cap. He tilted his head back to apply the drops, but the bottle stopped halfway to his eye. He remembered the bit about beauty products being made from mineral water taken from hot springs. "Everything from mud masks to eye drops."

He stretched forward, holding the bottle beneath the lamp on his desk. The label proudly proclaimed that it was "Made with pure water derived from deep in the Earth for the cleanest, most natural eye care available."

Shaking the bottle, he found it half empty. He drew in a deep breath and blew it out slowly, calming his nerves. He went through three or four bottles of the stuff a year but couldn't remember when he'd bought this one.

He tossed the bottle onto his desk, intent to take it to the lab in the morning. He sat back in his chair, rubbing his eyes with his fingertips. Dropping his hands to his lap, he stared up at the ceiling and began to wonder what his dominant trait was.

## From a Speaker, Blaring

## Jonathan Inbody

"Well Charlie, no one's sure how Biaregg's Disease started, not really, even if they tell you they are. There have been some theories ranging from the ordinary to the ludicrous, but to tell you the truth, none of these so-called experts have any more information for you now than they had two years ago."

"But is it contagious? Genetic? Venereal? Airborne?"

"If anyone knows, they're not telling. There have only been ten confirmed outbreaks, among a smattering of isolated cases, but until we have more information there's nothing any of us can do except…"

Caroline switched the radio off and merged into the left lane, going slightly above the speed limit to pass the slow sedan on her right. She couldn't be late, not today. She couldn't do anything that would draw any attention. She needed this job - the money, the car, her small apartment - and she had run out of sick days as of yesterday.

It was a shame they didn't give her any vacation.

She pulled into the complex's parking lot,

scanning her badge at the gate, then turned into a parking spot and turned off the engine. Her hand went up to her neck, checking to make sure the thick gray scarf she had wrapped around the bottom of her throat was still on tight and in the right position, and when she was satisfied she stepped out into the parking lot.

She could hear the sounds of morning in the city all around her; distant honks and puttering engines, yells echoing off of ungodly tall buildings, unseen birds chirping as a soft wind rushed past. She tried to focus on it, use it to tune out the sound of her heart beating, but she could already feel anxiety bubbling up like stomach acid at the back of her throat.

She gave a polite smile and a nod of recognition to the security guard by the door, then stopped at the rack to hang her coat before continuing into the office. As soon as she walked through the door the overlapping voices hit her like a wall, bouncing back and forth and filling every inch of open air in the call center as she walked briskly to her desk, eyeing her coworkers as she passed them and hoping desperately to avoid notice.

"Hey Cee!" Russell called as he walked out of the break room, stirring milk into his coffee with that smug fucking look on his face. "What's with the scarf?"

"I get cold," Caroline replied quietly.

A low, muffled noise came from inside the scarf and the fabric rippled slightly around her neck as something moved underneath. Russell furrowed his brow, changing his path to follow her as she kept walking.

"Cee?" he asked. "Cee? Caroline?"

Caroline stopped, hair raised on the back of her neck. Jess moved to intercept, rising from her desk to stand between them as Russell approached.

"What are you doing, Russell?" Jess asked flatly, folding her arms.

"Something's going on," he replied suspiciously. "She's hiding something."

Jess turned to look at Caroline, still facing away, then looked back at Russell. "Just contempt, I think."

Russell took an irritated breath in and slowly let it out. "Listen, I'm serious. She's…"

"Just give it up, man," Girard called from his desk, pushing up his headset microphone as he rolled back in his chair. "It wasn't enough for you to talk shit about her while she was sick? Now you've got to do it when she's here too?"

"That's not…" Russell sputtered. "This isn't…"

Martin leaned his head out of his office, eyeing Russell, Jess, and Caroline. "Is something going on out here?"

Russell nodded, moving to step around Jess as she moved to block him. "Actually, I'm glad you're here, Marty, because Caroline's…"

Jess scoffed. "Caroline's *what*, Russell? Wearing a scarf you don't like?"

"No," Russell replied, quickly sticking an arm out to reach past her. "She's *hiding* something!"

He grabbed the dangling end of Caroline's scarf

and she flinched, pulling the scarf off her own neck as she reared back to get away from him. Russell's eyes widened as he clutched the scarf in one hand and dropped his coffee with the other. Jess turned after him, then her face went pale as she caught sight of Caroline.

"What?" Caroline asked.

Girard stood up from his desk. "Is that…?"

A small, toothy mouth ran a scabby tongue over its lips, sitting where it had grown at the base of Caroline's neck, just above her collarbone. The pale, chapped lips seemed to quiver as the indistinct teeth grinded back and forth across each other, and the whitish tongue flitted back and forth behind them as everyone stared.

"I've been lying to everyone," the mouth said in a rough, nasally voice. "I've been hiding things from you!"

Caroline's hands shot to her throat, muffling the second mouth as her coworkers stared in horrified shock. She could feel the chapped lips sliding along her fingers, trying to push their way through to the open air, and when they realized they were trapped the mouth opened and began to tickle her palm with its tongue.

"What…?" Girard asked, his face losing its color. "What the hell *is* that?"

"What was it *saying*?" Russell replied, staring bug-eyed as Caroline took a frightened step back.

Jess reached out towards Caroline nervously, eyeing Martin from where he was still leaning out of his office watching them. "Caroline… is everything okay?"

"No!" the mouth on Caroline's neck answered, its raspy voice muffled behind her clasped hands. "There's something horribly wrong with me, and now there's going to be something horribly wrong with all of you!"

Caroline's eyes welled up with tears as Jess stepped towards her.

"I'm sorry," Caroline said waveringly. "I didn't mean... I tried to..."

"I looked up my symptoms on the internet!" the second mouth chimed in. "Zero results! I'm probably dying, and almost certainly terribly contagious!"

Russell gagged and covered his face, pinching his nose closed as he stumbled back past Girard. Jess yanked her hand away from Caroline and pulled the front of her shirt up to cover the bottom half of her face.

"What do you mean 'contagious', Caroline? Where did that thing come from?"

"It just... it just g-grew there, the day before yesterday," Caroline stammered as tears rolled down her face. "I tried to bandage it up, I tried... I tried to sew it shut, but it won't... it won't go away."

The mouth on her neck let out a high-pitched giggle.

"But if that's..." Russell started, sliding an office chair in between him and the others. "Why the *fuck* did you come in today?!"

Caroline sobbed. "I'm out of sick time! I really

need this job, and I thought… I thought I could just keep it covered up! With all the phone calls, I didn't think anyone would hear it!"

"Jess texted me to tell me that you were trying to get me fired," the second mouth added matter-of-factly. "Russ the Cunt's always spoiling the fun!"

"R-ru…" Russell sputtered. "Russ the Cunt? Do… do you guys call me that?"

Jess shrugged. "I think it fits. Don't you?"

Russell looked over at Girard, who winced and looked away.

"Well if you're sick," Martin said from his office door, "you'll have to take an unpaid vacation until you're better!"

Russell whirled. "What? Have you *seen* this? She's not sick; she's a freak!"

"She's not a freak!" Jess cut in angrily.

A scab on the side of Jess's neck tore open to reveal a pair of pale pink lips just in front of two lines of malformed teeth.

"*I'm* the freak!" her new mouth said chipperly. "I touch myself in the bathroom at work!"

Jess's eyes went white and she clutched her neck, quickly moving away from the others as she backed towards her desk. Their eyes followed her.

"Is that true?" Girard asked.

"No!" Jess yelled, pushing her neck down into her shoulder to muffle her second mouth as it started to speak again. "Of course it's not!"

Russell laughed, almost doubling over as Girard pushed past him.

"Okay, we need to call someone," Girard said

seriously, gesturing over at Martin. "This is fucked up; you two need to go to the hospital."

Jess and Caroline swapped a terrified look. All around them, the room had gone deadly silent, and they could feel endless pairs of eyes staring at them from every desk in the office.

"This is…" Girard stammered anxiously. "If it's contagious, then… then it's not safe for you two to be around anyone else."

Martin slammed his office door and locked it.

Russell dialed his phone and held it up to his ear. "Hello? Yes, we need an ambulance, maybe the police."

He coughed and something moved behind his tie. Two pale lips pushed up past his collar, a scabby tongue stretching out towards the phone receiver.

"Definitely the police!" Russell's new mouth added. "I've been stealing people's lunches from the break room!"

Russell slammed the phone down and grabbed his throat, feigning another cough as he started to back away.

"You're sick too, aren't you?" Girard asked fearfully.

"Only if kleptomania is a sickness!" Russell's second mouth replied.

Caroline's eyes scanned the office in a panic. All over the room, people were gasping, coughing, clutching at their necks and trying to drown out the cacophony of a hundred new voices, each one saying something its owner didn't want the world to know.

"I poked a hole in my boyfriend's condom!"

"I bully kids on the internet and encourage them to kill themselves!"

"I think vaccines cause autism!"

"What's happening, Caroline?" Jess asked fearfully. "Why did you do this to us?"

"I didn't mean to!" Caroline replied with a sob.

Jess turned to Girard. "Girard! Hey! You don't have one, maybe you're immune! Go get help!"

"I can't leave now," Girard replied. "What if I'm a carrier? I can't spread it!"

A sudden, blaring alarm sounded through the office, making everyone clutch their ears as the PA system buzzed to life.

"I'm sorry, everyone," Martin's voice said from the mounted speaker near the door. "Some people from the government came here last month to... to tell me that this might happen, that things like this have *been* happening - they said it happens more often in places where there's a lot of talking. They told me to put magnetic locks on all the doors, or... or they'd shut me down under a health code violation."

Someone at the far end of the office ran for the exit and frantically pushed the crash bar, but the door didn't budge.

"If everyone just stays calm..." Martin continued over the PA, "we'll be out of here in an hour or two. They gave me a number to call..."

Another voice, this one higher-pitched and raspy, interjected over the speaker. "I've been listening to all of *your* calls, by the way, especially your personal ones! I know more about some of you than your family does!"

Then, there was the sound of a brief scuffle, of Martin grunting and clothes rustling, and finally the PA went dead. For a moment, no one moved.

"Oh God…" Girard said sadly, his head in his hands. "I can't handle this right now; I just want to go home and pet my cat."

"Did I say *my* cat?" a raspy voice asked from under his turtleneck sweater. "I mean my neighbor's cat! I stole it and she thinks it ran away!"

Girard cringed, silently dropping back into his chair as his face turned red.

Russell rolled a stack of papers into a cone and shoved it into the mouth just over his collarbone, wincing as it sputtered and choked.

"No, don't!" Caroline yelled. "You'll…"

Russell suddenly screamed, pulling the roll of papers out of the mouth with one hand as his other one rose to clutch his neck.

"It opens up into your throat," Caroline explained, avoiding his eyes. "It uses your vocal cords; that's why it talks with your voice. The only way to stop it from talking is to suffocate yourself."

"We're all going to die!" the mouth on her neck added gleefully. "And it's all because I lied to you! I've lied about a lot of things, actually; half my resume is just stuff I made up! I never even went to college!"

Jess's eyes widened further. "Oh my god, is that *true*?"

"At least mine wasn't about masturbating!"

Caroline shot back.

"That's not even the best part!" Jess's new mouth replied happily. "When I masturbate in the office bathroom, I think about *you*! This one time, I saw your underwear a little when you bent over, and…"

Jess yanked the front of her shirt up to cover her neck and held it tightly in place, running back to her desk with her eyes fixed on the floor.

"Sometimes, I spit in people's lunches and put them back in the fridge!" Russell's second mouth said as he rushed for something to cover it with. "And I have herpes!"

"I've stolen *lots* of pets!" Girard's new mouth added from under his sweater. "Cats, dogs, gerbils - even a couple of fish! No one could love them like I do!"

Caroline paced back and forth as the room exploded into chaos all around her. People loudly argued and others dove for cover, while some pulled coats over their heads or screamed to drown out their new, hideous voice. A pair of paranoid people near the door backed away from their groups and bumped into each other, then turned and began to scuffle, sending a wave of fear and anger rippling across the room.

"Stop it!" Caroline yelled, stomping ineffectively on the carpet as she pushed her arms out at her sides. "Stop listening to them! Plug your ears!"

She ran over to Jess, shaking her shoulders as Jess buried her face in her hands.

"Jess, please! You've got to help me calm

everyone down!"

Jess frantically shook her head. "I can't! It's humiliating, I'm…"

"Do you want to know what's humiliating?" Caroline's second mouth interjected. "Humiliating is being so ashamed of your past that you steal a dead girl's identity!"

Jess's face shot up out of her hands. "What?!"

"She was dead when I found her," Caroline's second mouth continued, "Lying in a dumpster with a needle in her arm and foam all around her mouth! I took her ID, then broke into her apartment for all the other paperwork I needed! My name's not even Caroline!"

"That's not true!" Caroline shrieked, batting at her neck in a sudden, overwhelming panic.

Jess rose from her chair. "It's not? The rest of it was true, why wouldn't…?"

"I know, I know!" Caroline snapped back. "But it's not true! You have to believe me! The rest was, but this isn't, I swear to God!"

"But that doesn't make any sense," Jess replied warily, stepping towards Caroline. "Did you…? Are you lying to me?"

"No!" Caroline replied, shaking her head vigorously. "I swear I'm not! I swear!"

A hand shot out and grabbed her wrist, then roughly pulled her over to a desk. She whirled to see Russell towering over her, his tie loose and askew to reveal the disgusting pale mouth underneath.

"What kind of a psychotic bitch…?" he started,

glaring down at her.

"It's not *real!*" she screamed back. "It's lying!"

"You want to talk about psychosis?" Russell's second mouth suddenly asked. "*I'm* psychotic! I don't just spit in people's lunches when I'm not stealing them, there's someone in the office that I've been slowly poisoning!"

"Jesus Christ!" Girard blurted out, pulling Russell's arm away from Caroline. "What the fuck is wrong with you?!"

"It's a lie!" Russell snapped back as he grabbed Girard by the collar. "It's bullshit!"

Jess grabbed Caroline's hand, then half-dragged her across the office as they ran towards the door to the stairwell.

"It's locked! Everything's locked!"

"There's got to be something still open!" Jess replied, her voice rising into a panic. "We can't just be trapped in here!"

"Trapped?" Jess's second mouth added. "What a coincidence, I want to kidnap Caroline and keep her trapped in my basement!"

Caroline reared back, pulling at her arm as Jess held on. "No! Oh my god, no! Don't touch me!"

"It's not true!" Jess screamed. "You just said so yourself! It's lying!"

"I love Caroline sooooo much…" her new mouth continued, "I watch her through her apartment window all the time, and that's why I'll never let her leave me! We'll be happy together forever, and if she ever tries to escape then I'll just cut off her legs! After she's dead, I'll get her taxidermied and put her in a wedding dress!"

Caroline kicked at Jess's legs and scratched at her face until she let go, then tore off across the carpet at full speed to get away from her. She collided with Girard's back and bounced off into a cubicle, breaking a rolling chair in half as she fell through it.

He moved to help her, extending his arms to pull her back to her feet.

"Eating other people's pets makes me feel like a god!" the mouth on Girard's neck shouted excitedly. "It's the only way to make sure they'll be with me forever, and they're delicious!"

Caroline screamed and thrashed, wriggling back into the corner of the cubicle in a blind panic. She could hear screams all around her, thrown punches and torn clothing, and within seconds the entire office had descended into violence. Chairs were splintered, desks split, and bones broken, and the PA system hummed back to life.

"Look, I know that this is all very disturbing," Martin's voice droned through the speaker, "but there's really no cause for this sort of panic. There's no reason for anyone to do anything rash!"

"And by the way," his other voice chimed in, "check your credit scores, because I've been opening a shit ton of accounts using your names and social security numbers! I even use real personal information about you for the security ques…"

The PA system turned off again.

Russell ran past the cubicle carrying a chair as Caroline shrank back, and after a second she heard the unmistakable noise of him smashing it against one of the doors. Somewhere else, she could hear Girard begging for his life as a group of their coworkers surrounded him, intent on avenging the pets he had supposedly eaten.

Jess crawled into the cubicle and Caroline screamed, kicking out at her to keep her back.

"Shh! Shh! Stop it, I'm trying to help!" Jess whispered harshly. "Hey! If we get into Martin's office, we can unlock the doors!"

Caroline stared at her suspiciously. "How do I know you're not going to kidnap me?"

"How do I know your name is really Caroline?" Jess replied.

"You'll just have to trust me," she said slowly. "We'll have to trust each other."

Jess nodded. "Now come on."

The two women pressed themselves against the cubicle's inside wall, sneaking glances at the office outside to look for an opening. Then, they army-crawled out onto the carpet, turning around overturned desks and zigzagging through squares of cubicles as they made their way towards Martin's office at the other end of the room.

They approached a fat man lying face down on the floor with one hand clutched to his chest, his body unmoving and face covered in sweat, but as they passed they could hear his second mouth muttering something about white nationalists sometimes having a point.

They passed the long aisle at the center of the room and Caroline turned her head as they crawled past, just catching a glimpse of a circle of people stomping on a woman trying desperately to protect her face before it was blocked out by the next cubicle wall.

Finally, the two women reached the office and got to their feet, cautiously jiggling the doorknob as they tried to look in through the closed blinds.

"Go away!" Martin's voice called from inside the room.

"Martin, you've got to let us in!" Jess yelled into the door. "Everyone's killing each other out here!"

There was no reply.

"Think about it, Martin," she said, pushing her face up against the glass. "Why would they give you their number and tell you to seal the building? Because they're going to kill us all when they get here! It's a coverup; they're not going to let you off the hook because you're *management*!"

After a moment, a shadow appeared behind the door of the dark office, and the lock clicked open. Jess shouldered into the door, knocking Martin back into a potted plant, then stepped over him and headed for the desk as Caroline slammed the door behind them.

"Are you sure about this?" Caroline asked. "It could be dangerous."

"More dangerous than waiting for them to show up and gas us?" Jess replied skeptically, shoving a stack of papers off the desk as she pulled the desktop keyboard over. She fiddled with the mouse, typed something, then looked over at Martin as he wiped dirt off his cheap suit.

"How do I turn it off?"

"I was trying to tell you before," he said, climbing to his feet. "I don't think I can. Not from here, anyway. Maybe you'd have more luck flipping a breaker."

"Where are they?"

"Uh, I'm… the basement maybe?"

"Well that doesn't really *help* us then, does it?!"

The door shattered as a chair sailed through, knocking Caroline into Martin's desk. Russell stepped into the room, pushing more glass out of the door as he brought his shoe up to step through, brandishing a bowling trophy in one hand like a club.

"It's amazing the stuff people keep at their desks," he said, spinning the trophy in his hand as Jess and Martin backed off. "I'll bet if I kept looking, I could find a knife or something, but I kind of like how hefty this thing is."

Caroline rose from the desk, cowering as he raised the statue over his head.

"You did this," he growled. "To me… to all of us. Now we're all freaks, just like you."

The mouth on Caroline's neck suddenly opened. "I just remembered I have mace in my pocket."

"What?"

Caroline's hand shot up, her thumb pressed all the way down on the top of a can of mace as it sprayed directly into Russell's face. He stumbled backwards, engulfed in a cloud of burning pepper, both mouths coughing and sputtering as his leg caught on the edge of the wooden door frame and he tumbled back through the shattered door.

He landed on the pile of broken glass with a sickening crunch, tears streaming down his face as he swore and gasped for breath. Blood trickled out from his second mouth, where the set of unfinished teeth had bitten off the end of his pale, scabby tongue.

The sprinkler system went off, showering the office with ice-cold water as Caroline and Jess made their way towards the front door, where a group of gathered employees were trying to force the locks open by using a table as a wedge. Finally, the door broke open and morning sunlight poured in as people poured out, scattering into the parking lot and running for their cars.

All at once, a hail of bullets rained down from a nearby parking structure, dropping the line of escapees to the pavement with a flurry of echoing shots. Jess and Caroline ran out into the parking lot, too late to stop before the door, and peeled off in the opposite direction for the next street over.

Another string of gunfire sounded out across the lot and Martin cried out, collapsing only a few paces behind them, and as they reached the edge of the parking lot Jess screamed for help. More shots rang out and she fell to her knees, then toppled forward and flattened to the pavement, a curving arc of gunshot wounds oozing blood on her back.

Caroline kept running, barely aware of the sounds of the chaos she was leaving behind, and she nearly collapsed when she emerged onto the next crowded street. She sprinted out into the road, pushing past confused people as she hailed a cab, and when she got one she climbed inside and told the driver to just start driving.

He did as he was told, quietly and confused, but as they reached the edge of downtown he looked up at her in the rearview mirror.

"Miss? If you don't mind me asking… where are we going?"

Caroline smiled, pulling the scarf she'd taken as she'd brushed past a woman on the street tight around her neck. She wiped the sweat from her forehead, shook out her wet sleeves and pant legs, then looked out the window at the distant hills of the countryside far beyond the city skyline.

"I don't know yet," she said finally. "Somewhere quiet. But for now, turn up the radio."

## The Plague Advocate

## James R. Coffey

Nearly six months had passed before we knew Satan had returned. But even as I watched my last darling daughter succumb to the same horrific affliction her Saintly mother and three beloved sisters had, I knew. I knew the High Priest of Sinners had returned to enlist the remaining wicked of the City of London to His hellish legion (much as God had extinguished the wayward souls of Sodom and Gomorrah to save them from Him). That it should happen to the progeny of a Servant of God was proof enough of His fanatical resolve.

Fatuous humans, we! What moronic idiots we've proved to be! We'd been warned once before--oh, y*es!*--that Satan perched in wait on our gilded gables! One hundred thousand souls were lost to that arduous, futile battle! But Satan's hunger is ravenous! His lust insatiable! And his relentless appetite for carnage absolutely diabolical!

Yet we fatuous humans hide our sin-pitted faces behind our walls and moats and fortified gates believing we can practice His perversions unnoticed. In anonymity! As if the names of this earth's sinners are not already deeply etched in His accused Black Book! How conveniently we forget that before His fall from grace His powers equaled those of our Lord—and they've only strengthened since, thanks to us! The guilt we share is beyond measure!

Even before the day of this *revelation*, eleven of my closest friends and family and seventeen of my flock had fallen to it. Day after day, hour by hour, the tell-tail signs—the hideous buboes on the groin and neck and armpits oozing pus and blood, the blistering fever and vomiting of brackish gall, the grotesque blackening of the fingertips—appeared in greater number. Parishioners no longer sought my intercedence as a Warrior of God but instead locked themselves inside their houses hoping to hide from its erratic attacks!

It was at this point that I realized I was somehow resistant to the Black Death's wraith. Be it God's protection or be it a fundamental disposition that made my body unpalatable, I walked among the dying and dead and was unaffected. And I knew without a doubt I'd been chosen by God to endure this new attack by the Prince of Darkness and become the rock upon which His kingdom will be rebuilt!

***

As the pestilence spread from commoner to aristocrat, the long-standing myth that purity of blood made for natural immunity was emphatically dispelled. Dukes, Marquesses, Earls, Viscounts, Barons and the highest-ranking officials of the Church of England fell one by one without pomp or circumstance; disposed of in the same debasing manner as common thieves and harlots, wheeled to the edge of the City and dumped into one of many mass graves. So quickly did these unfortunates fall once symptoms appeared that no time was left to react or prepare.

A testament to man's unwavering greed, the ever-present treachery lurking in the shadows saw the Black Death as an opportunity to rise in status far beyond their rightful station. The detestable nature of this venomous disease made it easy for social climbers to abscond with one's most valuable possessions, hurry one's death, or even commit murder to usurp one's position. Thus a time came when nobles and people of standing sought to design the final moments of their demise and defend their station. They commissioned a Plague Advocate to act on their behalf.

A Plague Advocate's primary duties were to stand guard over the individual during the final stage of the disease, see to it that he receive the burial of his design, and deliver specific signed and sealed documents to the proper authorities outlining the succession to their particular office, how their estate was to be administered, and designate who was and was not to benefit from their assets. As a vicar and functionary of the Church of England of the highest standing, my reliability to function in this capacity was unimpeachable. And since I could not prevent nor stem the onslaught of this disease most vile, I saw it as my moral, God-sanctioned duty to tend to the fallen victims in the only manner now suited to me. My Church became the Plague-stricken City of London, my parishioners the dying and dead.

Vested as I was as I made my way about the City in the garb common to my trade--waxed fabric overcoat, mask with glass eye openings and a beak-shaped nose stuffed with herbs, straw, and spices to mask the horrific stench of the dying; few recognized me as I passed them in the street. While some of those I hesitantly refer to as my "colleagues" offered a variety of concomitant services for an additional fee (cures and remedies such as bloodletting and application of frogs, leeches or chopped-up snakes to the buboes to "re-balance the humors") my business was more *sagacious*. Except for hearing Confession or granting Absolution, I neither suggested nor emoted any desire to prolong my charges' lives. Considering the alacrity with which the disease lay waste the body, prolonging the suffering would be an abomination. The only humane course of action was to provide the dying the comfort of knowing their wishes and affairs would be carried out as they themselves would.

I began most days making my rounds of the charges under my care, monitoring the progress of the disease. And though it made no particular difference to me, the comfort I provided the dying was far more lucrative than the solace I'd provided the living low those many years.

Invariably, the service I provided required me to form many uneasy alliances within London's seedy underbelly, including embalmers, grave diggers, hackney-carriage drivers, casket makers, and on rare occasion, street thugs willing to defend home and property for a monetary reward. Loyalty and dependability being the overriding criteria, I found that in most cases money could guarantee both. For a few extra shillings the removal of a body, delivery to the embalmer, transport to the gravesite, and full interment could be performed as smoothly as the workings of a fine pocket watch.

The service I provided also required me to form uneasy alliances with a number of London's less-than-reputable City bureaucrats including magistrates, aldermen, and Officers of the Court who, for a few extra pounds in their purses, would dispense with the astringent regulations typically associated with disposal of plague victims. After two months in this business there were seventeen such *specialists* on my register.

***

By July of 1665, the Black Death ran rampant throughout the City of London. Those who had the means fled the City--including King Charles II of England, his family and his court, who left for Salisbury. London aldermen and most other city authorities were paid double to stay at their posts; the Lord Mayor of London, Sir John Lawrence, to his credit, deciding his rightful place was with the City. The most profound exodus came from business owners, merchants and professionals who closed their doors and fled, most opening new businesses in parts of England as yet uninfected. For several days a constant caravan of wagons, carts and coaches laden with possessions and goods carrying women, servants and children accompanied by horsemen was witnessed rushing away from the City.

By late summer, only a small number of fellow clergymen, physicians, and apothecaries remained to cope with the increasing number of plague victims, for which there was no remedy. Most of the poor had neither the means nor wherewithal to leave what little they had. Theirs was the greatest number of victims to fall.

In the spring of 1666 the British Department of Health calculated that at its present rate of destruction the Black Death would eradicate the entire population of London within five years.

(During the month of September 1665 alone, the Plague had killed 7200 people in a single week.) Convinced that the City's rat population were the obvious carriers of the disease (having likely infected the City's dog and cat population as well), a sanctioned killing spree was mandated by the City Corporation whereby a bounty of two pence was placed on each dead rat presented, prompting a City-wide extermination frenzy not seen since the London Witch Hunts a century before.

For weeks to follow, deranged hordes of drunken torch-wielding rat hunters trampled wildly through the streets of London, clubbing to death any small creature that moved—including 40,000 dogs and 200,000 cats, as well as several children--all heaped into two-wheeled death carts dragged to the outskirts of the City where bonfires burned day and night, forming a monstrous black cloud that hung ominously over the City, blotting out the sun and moon.

This, mixed with the abominable stench and fumes rising from the abscessed bowels of the City, collected and spread like a sickly, suffocating fog that made leaving one's house a veritable death sentence. And though millions of rats (cats and dogs) had been exterminated, it took only a few days to realize that Satan's Blessing still raged on! In fact, the death toll climbed! Making matters more unbearable, billions of fleas took to the air in massive swarms, seeking new hosts on which to feed. Attacking in terrifying numbers, these insects inflicted searing-hot bites that left hideous purple welts that swelled, blistered, and burst open! In the week following the vermin extermination, over 4000 known deaths occurred. Four of those deaths were my charges.

As desperation deepened, many Londoners who hadn't considered leaving the City before now sought to escape the Plague—even if it meant abandoning all their worldly possessions. In response, the City of London required that any citizen (commoner or Noble) desiring to leave must subject themselves to a 40-day quarantine to receive a Certificate of Health. Those manifesting the symptoms of the illness during quarantine were taken directly to a death house at the edge of the City and left there to perish. Since all surrounding cities and countries required a Proof of Health Certificate to enter, even if one managed to sneak out of the City, they would be barred from entering others—no matter their social station.

Counterfeit and poorly forged certificates became as readily available all over the City as tallow candles. On many occasions I was approached to obtain legitimate (back channel) travel documents for an exorbitant fee but I stayed true to my moral convictions. Without a doubt there were many less scrupulous City servants who had no moral qualms about allowing the death sentence to be carried to other cities. A major shift in the balance of London's wealth was taking place and many were blinded by opportunities they simply did not have the inner fortitude to resist.

***

By Whitsunday of that year both my reputation and purse had grown enormously. As most of my colleagues had themselves succumb to the Black Death, there were fewer and fewer of us offering this type of resolution. My intimate involvement with the inner workings of the City made me one of the first to become aware of property and estate opportunities, sizable lots and entire buildings affordable to fewer and fewer of the populous. Within two months I was able to secure seven tenement houses in Bishopsgate and two sizable manors at Westminster. Though it may be months or years before they would be of utility value, as I fully intended to survive Satan's merciless carnage, even now their intrinsic value was incalculable.

Possessing the manor of a former Bishop or Magistrate carried clout comparable to those lofty offices themselves. And though I never aspired to be a man of property nor papers, it seemed God now demanded it. Additionally, in lieu of payment I began accepting property and land and so benefited in lesser housing as well. Those wishing to control their final moments but had no heirs to leave their property were happy to forfeit their worldly possessions to me, primarily, I would assume, for fear of facing death alone.

It was in August of 1666 that my most disdainful funerary request was presented me. A request I initially declined but then reconsidered. It came from a French Lord who'd lived in London for nearly five years, who had left France to escape the Black Death raging there only find it had followed him. One of the wealthiest men in the City, his reaction to the coming Plague was to seal himself and his family within the walls of his grand estate and wait for it to pass. In addition to himself, his two wives and their maidservants, and their five daughters and their attendants, the manor staff was seventeen in number and included cooks, kitchen maids, chambermaids, foot servants, housekeepers, and wait staff.

For nearly eighteen months (though three of the staff invariably chose to leave the manor) no one from the outside, plague-stricken world had stepped foot inside. The Lord of the manor had prearranged to have food and other supplies delivered twice a month, deposited in a small guardhouse adjacent the manor where further instructions would be posted, but locked from inside. Despite these measures, Satan easily penetrated this seemingly impregnable fortress and infected most of its occupants. By the time word reached me through the grocer, only the *Seigneur*, one of his wives, one of his daughters, and three of his servants as yet presented no signs of impending Death.

When I arrived at the manor at the predesignated hour, even from the guardhouse the horrific stench of Death was gut-wrenching. Through my herb-laden mask I could detect the various stages of decomposition taking place within the house. As I was to learn, as each member of the household succumb to the horrific symptoms, they were banished to the stone-walled catacombs in the subfloor beneath the manor. The horrendous mephitis of the place, emanating as it did from within this hot, cloistered space, I can only compare to the mass grave sites on the outskirts of the City. Closed up as they had been for weeks, Death had become an almost tangible entity. This was the first place I had been where Death was a dreadful *thing*.

As I was escorted through the manor to the *Seigneur's* chamber, I could see the various places throughout where Satan had delivered His lethal kiss. Like lifelike *tableaus* depicting death scene exemplars, it was apparent that one guest had met Death while serving the Lord of the manor his supper. One had met Death while carrying fresh linen down the hall to one of the chambers. One had met Death while sitting at the harpsichord, perhaps serenading another with a charming minuet to pass the time. No longer allowing anyone to approach closely, the *Seigneur* sat in a darkened corner in half shadow. He spoke clearly and directly to me:

"Zis is what I would like, *monsieur avocat*. As

you can see, death 'as come *a ma maison*. Zare is no hope for escape. Myself, my wife and daught*eau* will soon be taken by zis evil most horr*id*! Even now my most cherished daught*eau* suffers the first evidence zat her death nears. My wife cannot be far behind." The Lord paused and gazed out the window as if to refocus his thoughts, then continued. "It is my wish zat zis evil that now resides in zis place remain 'ere." I looked at the Lord expectantly, trying to grasp his meaning. Though I had been commissioned to perform a number of unusual tasks for a number of peculiar individuals in the past, I had never encountered the task he was willing to reward me handsomely to perform. "I 'ave in my possess*ion, monsieur,* a quantity *avocat*—uh, of Indian opium. I ask zat in my moments *final* you 'elp me consume zis drug and then burn zis house to ashes."

I hesitated a moment to make sure I'd heard him correctly. "Do I understand you to say that you want me to set this estate on fire with everyone in it?"

"*Exactement.* And you can name your fee, *monsieur avocat.*"

Again I hesitated, suddenly feeling trapped by the intense morbidity seeming to now engulf me as I stood there; but also the incredible sense of power the *Seigneur* asked me to assume. I could only liken it to the charge bestowed upon Christian soldiers of the Crusades to wield their swords against the infidels who claimed not the Lord Jesus as their savior.

"I'm most sorry, *Seigneur,* but I am afraid I cannot take part in something so *heinous.* So... ungodly! I make no judgment about how other men choose to live or end their lives, but as a Servant of God I cannot take it upon myself to desecrate the bodies of those not under my charge. I know not these people or their final wishes. I am sorry."

With that I left the manor as quickly as I could make my way through the menagerie and out to the busy street. It had been the most repressive and staggering encounter since becoming a Plague Advocate.

***

I'm not quite certain what made me reconsider this ghastly proposition, but something in the way of conscience or Divine intervention did. Contained in one horrific space were twenty-eight plague-ravaged bodies that should never see the light of day. Twenty-eight loathsome, stinking corpses carrying the Devil's Curse the very air of which could further feed the specter of Death. To ignore this opportunity, I realized, would be to chance quickening Satan's filthy grip. I dressed and went immediately to the guardhouse and banged on the locked opening. One of the last remaining servants, a girl of no more than sixteen, cracked open the door and peered out. Her face bore the telltale signs of Satan's kiss.

"I am here to see the Lord of the manor. If he is still alive, tell him the Plague Advocate is here."

Leaving then returning a few minutes later, she opened the door and waved me in. The disease had ravaged her face beyond the ability to speak. The odor she carried was disgusting.

"So, *monsieur*, you've reconsi*deaud*?" the *Seigneur* said, clearly struggling under Death's grip.

"Yes, I have reconsidered."

"As you can see, we 'ave no time to waste. On ze table are two box*es*. The larger one is full of gold coins. Take it wiz you, it is yours. In the smaller, the *teriyak*. My wife and daugh*teaus* are of no concern to you. They passed on yesterday. All zat remain 'ere are myself and zi downstairs maid. If you would fill zis pipe and light it, we can begin. You will find many oil lamps throughout the estate to use for what you must do. Please, let us begin."

Breaking off a large chuck of the black tarry dough, I rolled it into a loose ball and placed it in the mouth of a strangely engraved long brass tube. I held it to the *Seigneur's* lips and brought fire to it. He inhaled sharply and held the intoxicating smoke in his lungs for several seconds before slowly exhaling. "Again," he whispered.

Again holding the tube to his lips he drew even more powerfully, holding it in until the dark gray smoke forced its way out of his blood-caked nostrils. Nodding for a third draw I refilled the opening and held it to his blistered, pustule'd lips. As he drew in the thick pungent vapors of the drug, his eyes rolled back in his head and he exhaled audibly, smoke rushing from his gaping mouth. His eyes remaining shut, his head lulled back and he made no more sound. Whether he was still alive or dead, I knew it was my cue to perform my promised duty.

Dumping the contents of the coin box into my coat pockets I proceeded from chamber to chamber along the third floor, dispensing the contents of each lamp onto the bedding and floor. Down to the second floor I did likewise, continuing to the first, dripping a trail of oil behind me. Downstairs in the kitchen I found the maid on the floor before the hearth, lifeless, blood dripping from her eyes. Taking three oil lamps to the sub-floor I proceeded to the catacombs where I poured oil on several of the corpses and drizzled a trail of it back up to the entrance. There I withdrew a glowing punk from the cook-fire and dropped it on the floor. In seconds it ignited, sending fire across the floor which traveled down the stone stairs to the sub-floor and back on itself to the first.

As I exited through the guardhouse I looked up to see the second and then third floor burst into flames. Hurriedly crossing the thoroughfare, I watched as the entire manor became engulfed. Thick black smoke bellowed from below ground and wafted up through the floors, bursting through the roof with a muffled explosion the likes of which I shall never forget. The Lord's work was done.

By mid-October of 1666 the death toll throughout London dropped significantly, and by Lent fewer than 200 per week were contracting it—down from 7000 in September. That number continued to drop as Christmas neared, with death across London almost unnoticeable. The British Department of Health announced that if these numbers remain steady through to the new year, the Black Death may have ran its course, once again. To date, from a total population of 600,000 before the Black Death arrived, an estimated 68,500 Londoners had been smitten by Satan's sword within the space of two years.

As January neared, many in exile began to return to the City. Some shops reopened. Though the Plague lingered in certain districts of the City, most met their final death-by-plague in February. There was no further need of my services. The Plague Advocate performed his final advocacy act on January 24, 1666.

***

While the Good Lord may indeed work in mysterious ways, the Lord of Darkness does not. It has been said that the Devil came to Earth to "tempt" us all from the righteous path, but I disagree. We humans *need* no temptation to stray

133

from the righteous path. Since the Garden of Eden, sinning has been in our souls--just as the need to fornicate for the sheer pleasure of it. Satan needn't *teach* us to sin—we are *born* to sin!

But no matter how many times we call the Prince of Darkness down upon us by our blasphemous ways, we feign ignorance of the consequences. Lo, here in London, the City of Sin and Sinners, we have been smitten twice—yet no lesson was learned. If sinning were to come to a halt tomorrow on this earth, Satan would have no desire to walk among us! Nothing to *feed upon*! Nothing to gloat about in the face of God! Yet we continue. So shall we remain a City of sinners in a world of sinners, calling down the Prince of Darkness to deliver us from goodness and purity. From the righteous path. And when the Black Death comes to prey upon us once more, we will surely prove yet again what moronic idiots we, made in the image of God, truly are!

I'll be holding Mass this coming Sunday in my parish at 9:00 a.m. and have no doubt that every pew will be occupied.

## There Is No Zombie Outbreak!

### Josh Schlossberg

RONNIE BARSTOW started Chatspace group
*LIBERTY LOVERS AND FREEDOM FIGHTERS*

RONNIE BARSTOW added description
*A place for American Truthseekers to stop government tyranny during this so-called "zombie" outbreak. Don't tread on us!*

RONNIE BARSTOW added new member
BRUCE P. MERRIMACK
RONNIE BARSTOW added new member
SANDIE FRANK
RONNIE BARSTOW added new member
CRAIG CLEMENTS

RONNIE BARSTOW shared a post
March 4 at 7:41 PM
*With so much bullcrap floating around the lamestream media, it's time for all of us non-sheeple to spread the Truth, stand our ground, and make sure our country stays free as the day it was*

*founded.*

SANDIE FRANK commented
*Thanks so much for starting this group up, RONNIE BARSTOW. The fearmongering is out of control, and we don't have the luxury of looking the other way anymore.*

CRAIG CLEMENTS commented
*ITS ALL THEATER!! ONE OF THE LAST STEPS IN THE GLOBALIST PLOT!! ITS NOW OR NEVER PEOPLE!!*

SANDIE FRANK added new members PATTY RUSSO, MITCHELL STANISLAUS, SAMANTHA PRITCHARD

RONNIE BARSTOW shared a post
March 7 at 8:26 PM
*So now the authoritarian politicians and lying journalists have switched out "zombie"—as if anyone over ten years old was buying that—for "Acute Neurological Wasting Disease" or ANWD. Let me ask you guys, do you know a SINGLE PERSON who's turned? Like, anyone at all? Didn't think so!*

CRAIG CLEMENTS commented
*CRISIS ACTORS BOUGHT AND PAID FOR BY THE ELITE!! PENTAGON RAN EXERCISE IN*

*JANUARY ON EXACTLY THIS!! THEIR SEEING HOW MUCH THEY CAN GET AWAY WITH BEFORE THEY SEND US ALL TO DETENTION CAMPS!!*

RONNIE BARSTOW commented
*Right on, CRAIG CLEMENTS! Glad you're on our side.*

RONNIE BARSTOW added new member MARINA SCHULTZ

RONNIE BARSTOW shared a post
March 9 at 6:22 AM
*Check out this article from Datadump proving zombies are just a bunch of meth heads let out of rehabs and looney bins. Share the Truth, my friends, share it far and wide, and don't listen to a word otherwise!*
*Datadump.com*
**Documents Debunk "Zombie" Narrative**
*-by Shelley Marcuson*
*Datadump has secured several classified documents proving beyond a shadow of a doubt that the "zombie" propaganda being foisted upon an unsuspecting and gullible public is nothing but...*

CRAIG CLEMENTS commented
*TOLD YA!!*

BRUCE P. MERRIMACK commented
*Yet not a peep about it on network news…*

SANDIE FRANK added new members MARILYN AMBROSE, TYLER GLICK, WINONA PACKARD-LEURS, BARBARA DANBURY

SANDIE FRANK shared a post
March 10 at 7:04 PM
*One of the methies went after a gym class at my kids' school, and now they're shutting down the whole district. What am I supposed to do, quit my job and stay home all day? Lord, give me the strength.*

CRAIG CLEMENTS commented
*ALL GOING ACCORD TO PLAN!!*

RONNIE BARSTOW commented
*Sorry to hear that, SANDIE FRANK. Anything we can do to help?*

SANDIE FRANK commented
*Know any babysitters?*

WINONA PACKARD-LEURS commented
*Me me me me!*

MARINA SCHULTZ commented

*That's why I'm running for school board. The only way to take our country back is to start local. I hope I can count on your votes.*

RONNIE BARSTOW shared a post
March 13 at 8:19 PM
*So for two whole weeks we're supposed to stay home to "slow the spread?" The best way to slow the spread—of fear—is to turn off your damn TV!*

*Anyone else's spouse getting sucked into this? Colleen won't even talk to me about it anymore. Says I'm getting sucked into "conspiracy theories." Know what I told her? It's not conspiracy theory, it's conspiracy fact!*

SANDIE FRANK commented
*Like ALL businesses aren't "essential"!*

RONNIE BARSTOW commented
*Texas is nowhere as strict as up here. Leon Rust is refusing to shut down his factories and is even firing any employees who don't show up to work! We could sure use a lot more like him calling the shots.*

CRAIG CLEMENTS commented
*RUST = 1 OF THE LAST TRUE AMERICAN HEROS!!*

RONNIE BARSTOW commented

*I don't know about you guys, but I can't just sit at home all day with Colleen crabbing at me. How about a protest or something?*

BRUCE P. MERRIMACK commented
*Agreed. It's time we get our message out in the streets for some old-fashioned civil disobedience. How about Sunday noon in front of City Hall?*

SANDIE FRANK commented
*Heck yeah!*

CRAIG CLEMENTS commented
*100%!!*

SAMANTHA PRITCHARD commented
*I'll come down on my lunch hour.*

RONNIE BARSTOW commented
*AWESOME! Let's shut this shit down! Bring signs and stuff!*

MITCHELL STANISLAUS commented
*I'll be the one waving Old Glory! Sweet land of liberty, of thee I sing!*

RONNIE BARSTOW commented
*You guys are the best! Can't wait to see you all in the flesh!*

RONNIE BARSTOW shared a post
March 14 at 5:57 PM
*Even though it was just me and BRUCE P. MERRIMACK today, I think we woke up some sheeple. Didn't see any media—or zombies lol—but I'm pretty sure the politicians knew we were there. Let's keep building the momentum!*

BRUCE P. MERRIMACK commented
*At the very least it was good to catch up in person, RONNIE BARSTOW. Because that's the very thing they don't want us doing. They might try to ignore us now, but once we reach a tipping point, they'll have no choice but to drop the charade.*

CRAIG CLEMENTS commented
*SORRY I FORGOT!!*

BRUCE P. MERRIMACK shared a post
March 17 at 2:12 PM
*I'm sure you've heard our illustrious "Public Health" director telling us bullets won't work against the Zs—which the idiots are now calling "people experiencing vital-impairment"—so there's no reason for us to buy guns. Which of course means we should all do the opposite.*

RONNIE BARSTOW commented
*And I quote: "A well-regulated Militia, being necessary to the security of a free State, the right of*

*the people to keep and bear Arms, shall not be infringed." I repeat, SHALL NOT BE INFRINGED!*

**RONNIE BARSTOW** commented
*Just got back from three different box stores and they were all sold out. Gun stores shut up tight, too. Gonna try the pawn shop.*

**RONNIE BARSTOW** commented
*Got an old shotgun and three boxes of shells because that's all the old guy would sell me. Best head down there quick if you want to stock up.*

**SANDIE FRANK** shared a post
March 18 at 9:11 AM
*Got turned away from the grocery store today because I refused to put on any stupid body armor! Not only won't that nonsense protect you from the methies, you're actually MORE LIKELY to get bit since you can't run away!*

*Pretty sure this is all about bankrupting small businesses by making everyone buy online. Heck, my church is the only place in town still open that's NOT a big box store.*

**PATTY RUSSO** commented
*Of course our church is still open because God don't take no sick days. Not only aren't we requiring body armor at services—it's so divisive!—we're not letting anyone in wearing those*

*O is for Outbreak*

*dang straitjackets.*

CRAIG CLEMENTS commented
*THEIR TRYING TO TURN US INTO ROBOTS!!
BREACH OF THE NUREMBURG CODE!! WE
WILL NOT COMPLY!!*

RONNIE BARSTOW commented
*It's obviously about the guns, people. They've
been scheming for decades to take them away, and
now they've finally found their angle.*

MARINA SCHULTZ commented
*No, it's to indoctrinate the children. Which is
why I'm running for school board. Can I count on
your votes?*

BRUCE P. MERRIMACK commented
*Sadly, I'm afraid the answer is "d," all of the
above.*

RONNIE BARSTOW shared a post
March 22 at 4:39 PM
*Anyone heard from CRAIG CLEMENTS lately?
Messaged me last night that he got into a tussle with
some meth head outside the bar—I won't say which
one because Chatspace will probably try to get it
shut down—and he hasn't gotten back to me since.*

SANDIE FRANK commented

*Nope, sorry.*

BRUCE P. MERRIMACK commented
*Chatspace won't bother ratting out some bar for staying open, but they censor messages all the time. Only a matter of time before it happened to us.*

RONNIE BARSTOW commented
*Stopped by CRAIG CLEMENTS place. Lights were on, and I could hear him banging around inside, but he wouldn't come to the door.*

SANDIE FRANK commented
*CRAIG CLEMENTS is a big boy, I'm sure he's fine. The good Lord's watching over us all.*

PATTY RUSSO
*He sure is, SANDIE FRANK. "Yea, though I walk through the valley of the shadow of death, I will fear no evil: for thou art with me." PSALMS 23:4*

RONNIE BARSTOW commented
*SANDIE FRANK Of course CRAIG CLEMENTS is fine. Never said he wasn't.*

RONNIE BARSTOW shared a post
March 24 at 3:04 PM
*Check it out. Finally, a politician not afraid to stand up for the American people.*

*Currentscoop.com*
**Gov. Pulaski Bans "Hitlerian" ANWD Public Health Measures**
*-by Matt Selway*

*Georgia Governor Pulaski passed an executive order on Monday making it illegal for both state agencies and private businesses to require body armor to protect against attacks from people experiencing vital-impairment, despite some of the highest case counts...*

SANDIE FRANK commented
*Tears of joy. God bless this man and his courage.*

BRUCE P. MERRIMACK commented
*Sorry to break it to you, but Pulaski knows his order is unenforceable and will soon be overturned by the courts. He's just gearing up for a presidential run. Nothing to see here but more empty virtue signaling.*

MARINA SCHULTZ commented
*I won't be virtue signaling when I'm elected to the school board. I've got all your support, right?*

BRUCE P. MERRIMACK shared a post
March 28 at 3:13 PM
*Good to see the mainstream media reporting on our esteemed "Public Hoax" director backtracking*

*on the whole bullets-can't-kill-the-Zs propaganda. The old snake finally admitted it was all about making sure law enforcement had enough ammo.*

RONNIE BARSTOW commented
*This is HUUUUUUGE! Now American citizens know for a fact that their government has been lying through its teeth!*

*If this news won't get Colleen back from my stupid in-laws', I don't know what will.*

RONNIE BARSTOW added new member MARCUS JONES

MARCUS JONES shared a post
March 29 at 10:38 PM
*You fucking IDIOTS! After over a million dead, blood and guts in every town and all over the media, you're honestly still telling yourselves ANWD is a HOAX?*

*Open your goddamned eyes, you imbeciles! Zombies taking over the streets! Hospitals overrun with dead! Packing corpses into freezer trucks! WHAT PLANET ARE YOU LIVING ON THAT YOU THINK THIS IS ALL MAKE BELIEVE?*

*If you're not going to help, then PLEASE PLEASE PLEASE stay home, so when you turn you don't take out your whole neighborhood with you.*

RONNIE BARSTOW removed MARCUS

JONES from the group

RONNIE BARSTOW shared a post
March 30 at 7:48 AM
*Sorry about that wingnut, guys. Thought he was one of us, but he was just another ANWD cuck spreading more fear porn. I've deleted his lies and banned him permanently from the group.*

*I promise to be more careful about letting in new members. And to be on the safe side, I'm getting rid of anyone I don't know personally.*

RONNIE BARSTOW removed MARILYN AMBROSE, TYLER GLICK, WINONA PACKARD-LEURS, BARBARA DANBURY PATTY RUSSO, MITCHELL STANISLAUS, SAMANTHA PRITCHARD from the group

RONNIE BARSTOW shared a post
April 2 at 6:57 PM
*Linking to an article showing how hospitals are blaming ANWD for almost every death, including strokes, gunshots, and car wrecks!*
*USAPundit.net*
***Hospitals Get Federal Funding for Claiming ANWD Deaths***
*-by Thomas Harrington III*
*Whistleblowers at medical facilities around the country have exposed the widespread practice of hospitals attributing deaths from accidents and*

*natural causes to …*

SANDIE FRANK commented
*Every morning and night I get down on my knees and pray that these people will burn in hell for what they've done.*

RONNIE BARSTOW shared a post
April 6 at 8:11 PM
*A bit of a bummer to report, guys. Stopped by CRAIG CLEMENTS place again, and the mail was all piled up out front. Bad smell from inside. He forgot to lock his garage, so I snuck in.*

*Poor guy was wandering around in a daze, moaning like he was in pain, face covered in sores. Yep, I hate to admit it, but looks like our old pal got his dumb ass hooked on the meth. Wouldn't even talk to me about it, just chased me out real quick.*

*Left him a couple can of baked beans in case he gets hungry. I'll let him detox a bit and check up on him in a few days.*

SANDIE FRANK shared a post
April 11 at 1:44 PM
*And right on cue, they're trying to push some new "vaccine" made from aborted fetuses that changes your DNA. I even heard there's a microchip that tracks your movements. I'll die before I put any of that poison into my body or any of my family's. And kill anyone who tries to make*

*O is for Outbreak*

*me take it.*

RONNIE BARSTOW commented
*People have bought into the narrative so deep they've lost their minds. Father-in-law pulled a fucking gun on me when I tried to see Colleen this morning, screaming that I was "infected," and he'd blow my head off if I didn't leave! This is what mass psychosis looks like, people. I was hopeful for a while, but this keeps getting worse every day.*

BRUCE P. MERRIMACK commented
*Three guesses as to who's funding the vaccine...*

RONNIE BARSTOW shared a post
April 17 at 5:51 PM
*Sorry haven't posted in a while. Been trying to make sense of everything. And here's what I got.*

*Even if zombies were real—they're not!—just because SOME people get bit doesn't mean the rest of us can't go on living our lives, amiright? Pursuit of happiness, and all that, eh?*

BRUCE P. MERRIMACK
*No matter what the P.C. police say, if you check the stats, the only ones getting bit are the elderly, the chronically ill, and the overweight. Sorry, but if you're not healthy enough to get away from some brainless waddling meth head, you'd probably die of something else soon anyway.*

SANDIE FRANK shared a post
April 14 at 3:14 PM

*Know why they're pushing the "vaccine" so much? It's very simple. Because the actual cure is super cheap and available to everyone.*

*I'm linking to the latest Moe Hogan podcast where he interviews two biologists talking about a study showing 100% protection from ANWD after taking bisacodyl, which you can find in any pet store. People are getting banned from Chatspace for even talking about this stuff, which is how you know it's the real deal.*

*MoeHogan.com*

*Episode #1529: The ANWD Cure Big Pharma Doesn't Want You To Know About*

*Moe welcomes biologists Chet Rhine and Helena Beyer to blow the doors off the mainstream vaccine narrative by sharing a new study out of...*

BRUCE P. MERRIMACK commented
*And here's the study for any hater who says we're making this stuff up.*

*Viralload.org*

**Effects of a Single Oral Dose of Bisacodyl Canine Laxative Suppositories on Clinical Outcomes in ANWD Infected Subjects: A Pilot Clinical Trial in Kazakhstan**

RONNIE BARSTOW commented

*O is for Outbreak*

*There's still plenty of the suppositories left at the pet store. They taste like crap but get the job done. Picked up a bunch for myself and left a few doses outside CRAIG CLEMENTS house. Dickhead's still ignoring me, but I can hear him banging around inside, so sounds like he's doing okay.*

RONNIE BARSTOW shared a post
April 17 at 10:42 AM
*Anyone heard from SANDIE FRANK lately? She's not responding to messages or texts.*

BRUCE P. MERRIMACK commented
*Nope.*

RONNIE BARSTOW added new member KRYSTAL WAGNER

KRYSTAL WAGNER shared a post
April 19 at 11:19 AM
*Thanks for letting me into the group! I heard about what you folx were doing and had to join! Wanna be up front that I probably don't share your politics on most things, but I'm 100% with you opposing the vaccine.*

*Three words for how to stay healthy while this thing runs its course: Raw. Carrot. Juice. My whole family's been drinking nothing but for the last seven weeks, and we're all still healthy as horses (just make sure it's organic)!*

RONNIE BARSTOW commented
*Worth a try, I guess.*

BRUCE P. MERRIMACK commented
*No fan of veggies, over here lol. But to each his own.*

KRYSTAL WAGNER commented
*To each *their own*

BRUCE P. MERRIMACK shared a post
April 28 at 9:13 AM
*Even the mainstream media is catching on that this all probably started from a lab leak at the Bayonne Center for Virology in the south of France. But of course they won't let us talk about it because it's "xenophobic."*
*Washington-Tribune.com*
**Did ANWD Come From a Lab?**
*-by Olivia Bellingham*
*Two weeks ago, eighteen scientists wrote a letter to the journal Biology calling for a new investigation and describing both the animal-to-human theory and the lab-leak theory as "viable." The idea is made plausible…*

KRYSTAL WAGNER commented
*C'mon folx, this was no lab leak, it spread from eating escargot.*

RONNIE BARSTOW shared a post
April 28 at 10:33 AM
*Sure enough, the tyrants at Chatspace took down the Tribune article about the lab leak and gave us a "community strike," whatever that means.*

BRUCE P. MERRIMACK commented
*Boy, that was fast.*

RONNIE BARSTOW shared a post
May 3 at 5:18 AM
*Taking a trip up to my buddy Chuck's cabin in Montana for a week or so, one of the last places in the country that hasn't turned into a government-run nanny state. There's even a big biker rally next week that sounds like a hell of a lot of fun. Internet's crap up there, but I should be able to check in on my phone.*

*If someone wouldn't mind leaving some food out for CRAIG CLEMENTS, I'd appreciate it. I don't think he's been eating much, but he's still moving around in there, so hopefully on the road to recovery.*

BRUCE P. MERRIMACK commented
*Want some company, RONNIE BARSTOW? I can't say I'd mind some time away from the city, myself.*

BRUCE P. MERRIMACK commented
*RONNIE BARSTOW, I could drive us both up if you want. Got an extra fly rod, too, if you wanna do some fishing.*

BRUCE P. MERRIMACK commented
*You already leave, RONNIE BARSTOW?*

RONNIE BARSTOW shared a post
May 12 at 6:10 PM
*Hey fellow Freedom Fighters! Long time no chat! Been out deer hunting, horseback riding, and trout fishing with Hank. It's like frigging summer camp up here! I'm on a library computer right now—yep, everything's still open—so I could check in.*

*Colleen isn't returning my phone calls, so maybe one of you BRUCE P. MERRIMACK, SANDIE FRANK, KRYSTAL WAGNER, MARINA SCHULTZ could leave a note at my in-laws' (I'll DM you all the address) letting her know I'm okay and thinking about her?*

RONNIE BARSTOW shared a post
May 25 at 3:44 PM
*The meth heads have finally made their way up here, some of them from that biker rally, judging from all the leather. But instead of pissing their pants like the rest of the world, the locals are just learning to live with it. Might stay another week or*

*so just for the heck of it.*
    *BRUCE P. MERRIMACK, SANDIE FRANK, KRYSTAL WAGNER, MARINA SCHULTZ Anyone drop off that note to Colleen yet?*

RONNIE BARSTOW shared a post
June 4 at 1:27 PM
*Running a bit low on supplies since the bikers looted the supermarkets. How are things back in the city? Library's closed now, too, so I'm sending this from my phone. Can someone let me know if my posts are getting through?*

RONNIE BARSTOW shared a post
June 6 at 9:11 AM
*Hank went out fishing yesterday and still hasn't come back. Gonna go look for him. And BRUCE P. MERRIMACK or anyone else, if you've got food—cans and dry goods, especially—I can get you directions to the cabin.*

RONNIE BARSTOW shared a post
June 6 at 8:47 PM
*Found Hank wandering around in the woods. Looks like the idiot ran into some bikers because he was all hopped up on the meth. Dumbass was so high, he didn't even recognize me and wanted to fight. Even bit my fucking arm when I shoved him off. Not a bad wound, I cleaned it up just fine with some iodine.*

*I know it's Hank's cabin and all, but I'm not letting that asshole back inside until he stops taking that junk and cleans the fuck up.*

RONNIE BARSTOW shared a post
June 7 at 4:12 AM
*Looks like I got me a little case of the flu. Fever, chills, muscle aches, and all that fun stuff. But to be on the safe side I chewed up a couple of the suppositories.*

RONNIE BARSTOW shared a post
June 7 at 5:49 PM
*Goddamn I feel like shit. Keep puking up the suppositories. I just need to get some shut eye and I'll be up bright eyed and bushy tailed come tomorrow.*

RONNIE BARSTOW shared a post
June 7 at 9:08 PM
*cant sleep worst headache ever had feels like somene prying open skull with hndred chisels cant walk keep pising myself but dont even care love you colleen loveyousomuch*

RONNIE BARSTOW shared a post
June 8 at 1:32 AM
*hunbgryhmgryhugryhiungryungry*

**You are temporarily blocked**

*O is for Outbreak*

*This is your second warning for violating Chatspace's Statement of Rights and Responsibilities. You are now blocked from posting content on Chatspace for 48 hours.*

*If you continue to abuse Chatspace's features, your account could be permanently disabled.*

**Speak Easy**

**Lisa Zang**

## *Part One: The Second Outbreak*

Vibrations from a body hitting the ground spread through the asphalt under her feet. Another jumper. Another watermelon thump and the sound of expelled air. Who was it this time? Not that Lorelei knew people, even in this small town. Rather, she wondered who the jumper had been before they jumped, before they'd contracted the Pain?

"Hush, Crow," she whispered, to the little black dog at her feet, to his *errr*, to his slow and steady warning growl. "I know. It's okay. I heard it, too. It was only a jumper. We're okay, Crow." She tugged on the visor of her cap and tried to focus her eyes on the ground. Only on the ground. Only on Crow. But her eyes wouldn't open to let her see much. White paws. The white tips of pointed ears. A flash of white-tipped tail.

Optophobia her doctor called it, the way her brain tried to shut her eyes, the way her anxiety tried to shut out the world, but if she thought about

Crow, only Crow, not the horror, not the horrors that her eyes might see, not the possibilities of horror, then, maybe, she could get her eyes to open a bit more.

She bent to swing her hands around her feet, to get a hold of the little dog, to pick him up in her arms. "Shhhh. No more growling. Come here, Crow. You're not being a very good anxiety dog."

Lorelei didn't mind the night, but it was almost dark, and she wanted to get to Noah's. "Crow," she whispered. The dog's growl turned into a bark. "Stop, Crow. You're going to get us into trouble."

The dog yelped. He hit hard against her ankle, and her hands examined his folded body without looking at the man who kicked him. "You're okay, baby." Lorelei picked up the dog.

"He… bit… me," the man said, in a soft measured voice, his every syllable the same monotonous, middle-ranged tone as the syllable that came before it. No punctuation. No intonation. Every space between syllables the same. "I… will… take… him."

"Mayor West, I'm sure you have more important things to worry about. Your people are jumping out of windows." Lorelei mouthed the words without sound, instead of choosing to talk the Speak Easy. She was angry. She wanted to look angry. Speak Easy was too slow. She couldn't deliver the uniform one syllable speech and look angry at the same time. "Are you feeling the Pain?" she mouthed, implying his cruelty was the result.

"No… but… we… must… think… of… those… whose… ears… fill… with… Pain."

Hypocrite, she wanted to mouth. When had he ever cared about the people in the town? Commuters who traveled hours to and back from D.C. to live among mountains and rivers, to organize art fairs and music festivals, to find comfort in restaurants and neighbors, to jump out windows, to drown in rivers, to poison themselves. He'd been happy to take the credit for the accolades bestowed on the *Number One Most Livable Town,* giddy at seizing power from opportunity. The outbreaks presented opportunity.

"If… the… dog… can't… stop… bark… he… can't… stay… with… you… I… don't… care… how… fame… you… and… he… are… I… will… have… him… put… down."

Another watermelon thump and the sound of expelled air vibrated the sidewalk beside her. The mayor texted 911. No phone calls. No sirens to alert the public an ambulance was on its way.

"I… will… keep… him… from… bark… and… from… your… pant… leg," Lorelei said, but the mayor was texting again. A woman running down the road was screaming; her hands were holding her head. Screaming was against the law.

Lorelei bent to kiss the top of Crow's head and she felt the wag of his tail. "Let's get to Noah's," she whispered.

She walked three blocks, before making a turn onto the brick of the old town's pedestrian zone and its row of mom-and-pop shops. Closed for the virus. Reopened with fanfare after the virus. Now, closed again, with the Pain. There was no working with the relentless sound of a train running through your head, the brain-splitting pressure fluctuations of a tornado inside your ears, the unbearable high-pitched ringing, the painfully deep unearthly vibrations of a devil calling your death.

She passed the movie theatre, another soundless, captioned, movie publicized on its marquee. Words were too painful to have movies with sound. Normal speech was too fast for those who'd contracted the Pain. Normal-paced speech caused garbled, erratic pitches and rhythms. It caused confusing highs and lows. It caused agony and disorientation. Movies without sound were the law. People still needed entertainment, the president said.

She made a left onto cobblestone. The alley was quiet. No thumps. No screams. No tall buildings. Lorelei stopped in front of an old stone building that looked like it had once been a house. A wrought iron bracket attached to its stone supported a carved wooden sign that read *Noah's*. She didn't lift her head to look at the sign, but she knew it was there. She knew its letters were blue. She knew that below the name was a carved ark painted green and that beside the ark, stood two yellow giraffes. Planks of wood, nailed across the front door, warned *Alcohol Prohibited* in red paint. An official looking paper that began, *By order of the Federal Government* was pasted on the large window to the right of the door.

Lorelei put Crow on the ground and headed to the side of the building. "Ready to see Noah?" she asked. A steep stone stairway led to a cellar, and Lorelei took hold of its thin iron railing. At the bottom, there stood a heavy metal door with a digital lock. Lorelei keyed in the numbers, 230423110. 2304, for the date of Noah's flood, because Noah had read it somewhere online. 2 and 3 for B and C, and 110 for the days Noah lived on the ark – the 100 days of rain, and the added ten it took for the waters to recede.

The door opened and she and Crow stepped into the vestibule. She shut the door behind her, and she keyed in the code for the second door - 35000, the estimated number of animals on the ark. "The animals knew where to go for safety," Noah said. "I like to think that's why I'm here."

When Lorelei opened the second door, the little dog ran to behind a saloon-style bar, to a man who lifted him into the air. "Crow," said Noah. He looked just like Buddy Ebsen, same gentle manner, same voice, and because Lorelei never knew her own father, she imagined it was him. "Hell… o… love… ly… green… eyes." The words were her cue that it was safe. Nothing to fear, no something horrible about to happen. It was safe for her to open her eyes.

The imposing mahogany bar dominated the underground space. Noah had carted the thing with him from his old establishment in Wyoming but ended up storing it in the cellar. He had to saw the thing apart just to get it down there, but he'd put it back together for the speakeasy.

"A speakeasy during the Speak Easy," Noah said, when he told his customers he was going underground. "Drink and camaraderie are going to get us through this thing." Of course, it wasn't how the government saw it. Drinking contributed to depression, the president said, caused people to jump from bridges and water towers and buildings. "If... we... are... to... live... with... the... Post... vir... al... Pain... we... can... not... live... with... al... co... hol." It was the line from the president's speech, the speech re-enacting prohibition, that everyone repeated with the opposite spin.

"If... we... are... to... live... with... the... Pain," people said, "we... can... not... live... with... out... al... co... hol."

Lorelei took off her cap, shook out her hair, and opened her eyes all the way. She liked the speakeasy better than the bar upstairs. No windows. Noah kept the lights dim.

She pulled up a stool and Noah handed her Crow.

"You... o... kay... Lei... lei?"

"Two jumpers, a street screamer, and the mayor, on my way here," Lorelei mouthed in a half-whisper. Three people sat at the far corner of the bar, past five empty stools to her left, and there was a man and woman to her right, three barstools down. Card tables, a couple of which were occupied, were scattered among décor Noah brought with him from Wyoming. He'd hung iron cattle brands from the ceiling, mounted a moose head behind the bar, and nailed up a couple of antelope heads on the walls. A heap of old saddles that used to be seats for bar stools were piled up on the floor. Stacks of black and white photos of cowboy life graced the tops of some of the card tables. Secret compartments Noah built inside the wooden bar held the liquor being served to customers. A separate room, with a door that looked like part of the wall, served as storage for the rest of the alcohol.

Noah shook his head. He slid a vodka martini in front of Lorelei, and he leaned in. "Wonder if one of those jumpers was Danny," he whispered. "Danny wasn't looking too good when I saw him in the park this afternoon. He was holding his ears and shaking his head. I tried to use the Speak Easy, but he just wasn't having it. I thought Speak Easy was supposed to be soothing, distract from the Pain, keep people feeling socially connected. I should have made him come with me to the bar. Kept an eye on him. Speaking of keeping connected, I got the television working. Look. There you are. Your news station plays nothing but you and Crow. All day, every day."

Lorelei took a sip of her martini and looked up at the screen in the corner. It was her segment on the Great Allegheny Passage, the one in which a black bear came bounding across the trail in front of her and Crow. Viewers loved it the first time it aired - Crow hunkered down with his back end in the air, growling at the bear in defense of Lorelei. That was the one where Crow tried to herd wild turkeys, too.

News stations didn't play news anymore. Reporters tried to talk Speak Easy, but something about the way it came through the air waves, it had the same painful effect as normal speech. They tried captions only, but crews couldn't actively film anything, no matter how benign the story. A jumper would get in the shot, or someone would run through a taping holding his ears and screaming how he couldn't stand the Pain anymore. The government tried to keep that kind of thing from being seen. "You and Crow are even more famous now, than you were before. Rumor is other cities are asking for the Leilei and Crow shows. Is it true?"

Lorelei smiled. The show started out as an offbeat upbeat fluff idea she'd peddled for filler to markets in D.C. and Baltimore. She called the segment Leilei and Crow – a woman and her dog investigate nature and off-the-beaten-path attractions. She was lucky that a D.C. station picked it up. How else could she have made a living? The only time she opened her eyes fully, other than in her house, or at Noah's, was in nature and behind a camera. "Never seen anything like it to this extent," said her therapist, "but understandable given the circumstances." She didn't have a therapist anymore. She had Crow. She had Noah. She had her vodka martinis and the dark.

"Is Hugo stopping…" Noah mouthed. Then, "Hey… Hugo," he said looking up. The man coming through the door was tall and shaggy. His dark hair was tossed around his head, and a day's growth of beard shadowed his face. He looked too worn for a man in his thirties.

"I'll… take… a… shot… of… all… you… got."

"You… o… kay?"

"Now… that… I'm… here… with… you… two." He sat down next to Lorelei.

"It's safe," Lorelei whispered. "You can talk. Everyone else is whispering normally." Hugo looked around the room.

"Set your medical bag down. Relax, Hugo," whispered Noah, filling the shot glass in front of him with whiskey.

"How is it you still have whiskey?"

"Keep it for my special customers. The vodka, too." He winked at Lorelei. "Everyone else gets moonshine."

Hugo noticed Lorelei on the television. "Hey, there you are, again. Plays just as well without the sound." He smiled. "Remember when they brought you in to do the real news during the virus?"

"I made the mistake of explaining my anxiety."

"Mistake? What mistake? Viewers loved it. Highest ratings that station ever got, the way people tuned in to see you freak out. Your eyes getting all blinky. Your hands flying up to cover your face every time there was a video of something bad. Who knew those were the good old days?" He stopped. He downed the shot. He gave Crow a pat on the head.

"Your ears okay?" he asked Lorelei.

"Fine. Yours?"

"So far."

Noah poured a second shot for Hugo and set a glass of water in front of himself.

"It's bad," said Hugo. "It's..." Guttural sounds erupted into high-pitched agony as a man ran toward the bar from the door.

"It won't stop. Make it stop. I can't make it stop."

Noah stuck out his arm. "Sit... Dan... Sit... I... pour... you... a... drink."

Crow started a low rolling *errr*. Lorelei tried to scoot her stool away. Noah filled a glass quickly and pushed it toward the man, turning for just a second to grab a bar rag. Hugo got up to shut the open door.

It was one motion, the man's lean over the bar, grabbing the ice pick, shoving it into his ear. Lorelei heard the scream; she saw the ice pick sticking out from his ear. She saw him extract the pick and do it again. She couldn't breathe. She couldn't get air. The room filled with screams. He did it again and again and again. Lorelei held Crow. She closed her eyes. She was going to pass out.

"Shut him up! Shut him up!" yelled a man.

"I've got it Lorelei. I've got it. Everything is alright." Hugo's voice seemed far away; it floated on the other side of a mountain.

***

"He'll be out for a good long time," said Hugo.

Lorelei looked down to see she was still sitting on the bar stool. Crow still sat on her lap. How long had she been away? *Been away*, that's what she called it when she didn't pass out, but when everything inside her shut down.

"Are you okay?" It was Hugo. She wasn't okay. She set Crow on the bar, and she covered her eyes. "It's okay, Lorelei," said Hugo. He took Lorelei's hands from her eyes. "We managed to get a couple sleeping pills in him before Noah and I dragged him to the back. He's asleep on the cot." Noah put another martini in front of Lorelei and picked up Crow from the bar.

"Is it? Is it okay? Will he be okay?"

"Lorelei, this happens every day, probably a thousand times a day. People fill up my office begging me to poke out their ear drums."

"Does it work?"

Hugo shook his head. "My patients cut off fingers and toes, drill holes in their brains. They're desperate to take the Pain from their ears."

"Stop. Stop, Hugo. Stop." Lorelei's eyelids fluttered. Her heart pounded.

"You just don't see it, Lorelei. You know that." Hugo pointed to the television screen in the corner. "You only see *Leilei and Crow*. People are struggling out there, Lorelei."

"I know that." Lorelei put her hands over closed eyes.

"It's life. Our life. It's the world out there. For God sakes, Lorelei you're not eight years old. It's not your brother we're talking about."

"Stop," mouthed Noah to Hugo.

"People are choosing to kill themselves out there. They're choosing to kill each other. They've lost control."

"You've lost control," mouthed Noah. He pounded his fist on the bar.

"It's not a freak accident. It's not a fly-away table umbrella impaling your brother in his lounge chair."

"No!" said Noah.

Lorelei couldn't get air. She felt hot. She was choking. She was with her brother. They were on their sides, in their lounge chairs at the hotel pool. They were facing each other. They were joking around. Her brother was saying, "Knock, knock," when the wind picked up the umbrella, and speared the pole through his arm pit. Blood spewed. He couldn't move. He was pinned. He couldn't talk. His eyes looked at Lorelei, wide, frightened, asking what was happening to him, begging her. She wanted to scream, but she didn't scream.

Lorelei dropped her hands. Her eyes stayed shut. Noah put Crow in her lap.

"They can't keep up with the number of people trying to drown themselves. No pharmacies, no medications, because the government doesn't want the drugs used for suicides. Dan is lucky I hoarded those sleeping pills."

Lorelei stroked Crow's fur. *Breathe*, she told herself. She inhaled.

"I'm sorry, Lorelei. I'm sorry. I shouldn't have done that. I shouldn't have said those things. I just want you to be safe. I need to know you can take care of yourself." Hugo took her face in his hands.

Lorelei opened her eyes. "Not everyone gets Pain, though, do they, Hugo? We don't have it. I thought maybe some of us were immune."

"It doesn't seem that way, Lorelei." He laid one hand on top of Crow, and his other hand on top of hers. "If you contracted the virus, you will have the Pain, and everyone had the virus."

"When Hugo?"

"Well, the three of us got the virus all at about the same time, so, by my estimation, our Pain should start any day."

"Should I kill myself now?" She wasn't joking. Her heart pounded again. There was no air in the room.

"We'll figure this out," said Hugo.

"How long does it take before it gets bad?"

"From the onset? Everybody's different in what they can stand, but from what I've seen, it's two weeks."

"Who's lived the longest so far?"

"A man named Herbert Mirestone. Four months and counting."

"How?"

"I don't know. He's got some social media site on the internet."

"The government is letting him broadcast?"

"Guess so. I guess they figure it's a positive thing, because the man and his family are making the Pain seem livable."

"How does the Pain start, Hugo?"

"You know that feeling of pressure, the vibration you feel in your ears when you're driving with one window in the back rolled down? It starts like that."

"I've got that now," said Noah.

### *Part Two: Herbert Mirestone*

The little dog stood at the townhouse door ready for a Leilei and Crow adventure. He was so happy, so innocent. What was she going to do when she couldn't function? How was she going to take care of him? Any day now, and then she'd have two weeks left. Should she open the door and just let him go? He probably wouldn't leave her. She got on the floor and looked into his eyes. "I love you, Crow. We're going to figure this out." The little dog lifted a front paw and laid it on top of her hand. She picked him up and sat in front of the computer.

**Search:** *Herbert Mirestone*
*Longest living Pain survivor,* **longlivemirestonehope.com**

"We have our web page, Crow. We're going to do what Mr. Mirestone has done and you and I are going to be alright. We're going to be alright, Crow." Crow covered Lorelei's face with his tongue, and Lorelei clicked on the web address.

*Today's Update –*

*We are ready for death. We are tired and ready for relief. The Pain has stolen our reasons for life – our love, our joy, our friendships, and our purpose. Without hope, we have lived life to intolerance.*

*So that there is no doubt, we are all in agreement on this, my wife, Beth, and my three lovely children, Addie, my eight-year-old, Charlie, my twelve-year-old, and Matt, my seventeen-year-old young man. Our children have made us very proud over the course of their short lives, and we love each of them very much.*

*It is also with overwhelming sadness, but with much consideration, that we have decided to take our pets with us. I am sorry to be so blunt, but you who have journeyed with my family through the Pain, have, as you've said, appreciated my bluntness, my tendency to tell it like it is, so that there are no surprises in the actions and consequences of following the advice I write here. Animals, as you know, do not contract Pain. But Addie's cat, Violet, our Yorkie, George, and our Sheepdog, Martha, are not wild, they are trusting, and loving innocents and we fear they would suffer left to fend for themselves without their family.*

*Please look to previous posts for advice on how to live successfully to this point, but know that eventually, you, too, will succumb, so it is best to use your time to prepare.*

*This is my final message.*

*God bless your souls. God bless our souls,*
*Herbert Mirestone*

Lorelei looked down at Crow.

### Part Three: The Tin Man

Lorelei walked up to the bar and sat on the stool

next to Hugo. Crow ran behind the bar to see Noah. Lorelei was five days in, and the Pain was already excruciating. The pulp nerves of a toothache on fire throbbed in both of her ears. And the deprivation. No music. Not even the sound of her own voice. The sound of her own voice drilled a hole through her head. Only the expectation for more pain.

She watched Hugo's lips meet the edge of his shot glass – Batman lips, Val Kilmer Batman lips. She should have said yes to sex. She should have had sex when they could both hear their sounds. Before Pain consumed her sensations.

She'd stocked up on food for Crow. She'd filled the townhouse with plates and bowls of Crow's food because the Pain might make her forget to feed him, might make her incapable of thinking of him.

She'd taken him on outings. She filmed them like before, but she didn't talk. She avoided bridges and water and tall buildings. She avoided hardware stores where a plethora of weapons could be found. The president hadn't thought of that. He hadn't thought to shut down the hardware stores.

She touched Hugo's wrist. A deep oozing blister on the inside of his arm, on the soft skin just below the crook of his elbow, red and raw, showed from underneath his unbuttoned shirt sleeve. "What... is... this?" The Speak Easy banged through her head.

"Water," he mouthed. "Burned... with... water." He reached for a napkin, he pulled a pen from his shirt, and he wrote: *Scalded my arm to stimulate endorphins. Big injury = big endorphin release = lessening of background (chronic ear) pain.*

Lorelei lifted the sleeve of her left arm. Just below her elbow, in the same spot, Lorelei wore a wide rubber band to snap against her skin. It was a Herbert Mirestone suggestion: *Use a blade to cut into the soft underside of your skin beneath your rubber band when the Pain in your ears gets unbearable. This will increase the pain of your snap and will redirect the Pain from your ears.* Lorelei had two slice cuts beneath the rubber band on her arm. She snapped the rubber band, and let the sharp sting – a wasp sting, a venomous snake bite - shoot up and down her nerves. Noah placed a martini in front of her, and Lorelei gulped the drink down.

A second rubber band around her right thigh, hidden beneath Lorelei's pant leg, rubbed against two wounds she'd cut this morning. She'd cut them with a saw-toothed steak knife. The steak knife hurt more than the clean-edged blade she'd used to make the incisions on her arm. The wounds from the saw were wider, deeper, they were jagged, more open.

"How... did... you... know... we... were... here...? Who... gave... you... the... codes?" Noah was talking to an older man who'd just walked into the cellar, a stranger who'd pulled up the stool next to Lorelei. Tanned skin. White hair. A white shirt. Khaki pants.

"I... am... a... mine... er... mine... ers...

good… at… dig… for… what… they… want…
I'll… have… what's… on… tap."

"Got… no… thing… on… tap… for… strange…
ers." Noah handed Crow to Lorelei and poured the
stranger a moonshine.

"Jack," said the man, and stuck out his hand.
Noah didn't return the handshake. He didn't look at
the man. He looked at a note from Lorelei, instead,
written on the back of Hugo's napkin. *Even Speak
Easy painful.* Hugo and Noah both nodded.

*Who said Speak Easy was soothing?* wrote Noah,
below what Lorelei had written. Lorelei pointed to
the president on the television. Was it a new
speech? An old speech? *Hang in there everybody,*
read the caption on the screen. *Poor choice of
words*, Lorelei thought.

The old man, Jack, rolled a silver pen in his hand
and pushed a cowboy photo across the bar in front
of Lorelei. Three cowboys - two sitting, one
standing, the one standing resting his hands on the
shoulders of the other two, button up shirts, wide-
brimmed hats on all three. Lorelei flipped the
photograph to the backside. *The government is lying
to you,* read the message. Lorelei passed the
message to Hugo, who pushed it past Lorelei to
Noah. Noah slid it back in front of the man.

*I had a flying dream,* wrote Noah, on the back of
a new napkin. *It felt good. I think jumping will feel
like that.* Even below his beard, Lorelei could see
Noah's face looked corpse-like, drawn, hardened to

the expression of being buried alive.

*No!* wrote Lorelei. I *need you, Noah. Your* daughter *needs you. Your daughter's new* baby *needs you.*

*The government is taking away babies,* wrote the old man on the back of his cowboy photo.

Lorelei looked up to see the man was nodding. The others read the message. Lorelei wrote, *Why????*

*Babies born after the virus won't get Pain. Afraid their suicidal parents with Pain will kill them. Government is collecting and raising the next generation.*

*Who will raise them? Everyone will have Pain.*

The old man shook his head. "Not me," he mouthed. "Not," he pointed his head toward the television screen.

He was right. There'd been no mention of the president having Pain. The President had gotten the fever months before Lorelei. He should have contracted the Pain by now. And Congress? No one from Congress had been reported having Pain. Were they all Pain-free? Were their families Pain-free? The president's advisors?

*There's a cure,* wrote the old man on his photo. Lorelei pushed the message over to Hugo. She didn't see Noah. Where was Noah?

*What is it? Where?* wrote Hugo.

*A new mineral. Discovered in mines. All over the country. You have a mine, here, in the woods.*

"A new mineral?" mouthed Hugo.

*Earth has more than 1,500 undiscovered minerals,* the old man wrote. *We brought the number down to 1,499.*

"Why should we believe you?" mouthed Hugo.

*Tomorrow, here, 7pm. I'll bring you each a sample. Put the mineral on your tongues. It works immediately, but you'll need one dose every day for a month to be cured. I can get you the rest of your doses later.*

*Why tell us?* wrote Lorelei.

*I'm a specialist,* he wrote. *When I object to a government project I'm working on, I leak it. My way of making sure I have a heart. Leaked Area 51, FEMA's building of secret concentration camps, deep state conspiracies.*

Noah was back behind the bar and Lorelei turned the photo so Noah could read the rest of the messages. Noah handed his phone to Lorelei.

A text message from his daughter read: *Dad, gov. trucks in the neighborhood. Blocking off streets. Say they're going to interview families for gov. research on Pain. Interviewing starts tomorrow.*

*Pack only what you need, Anna,* Noah responded. *Leave now! Leave on foot. Hide baby Eva in a backpack.*

*Dad! You live 50 miles away.*

*LEAVE NOW, ANNA! Don't take the main roads.*

The old man picked up the photograph from the bar and lit the paper on fire. "What is this project called?" mouthed Noah.

The old man wrote the word *Clock* on a napkin, and then lit the napkin on fire.

### *Part Four: Beating the Clock*

*Keep out* read the sign pasted to the second, inside door, but Lorelei keyed 35000 into the lock. She opened the door. Hugo was behind the bar, and he nodded to the pen and paper in front of him. It was easier than trying to talk Speak Easy.

*Noah?* wrote Lorelei.

Hugo shrugged. There was no smile. No one smiled. His hair hung over his eyes. His beard looked three days longer than yesterday. *Not here, yet,* he wrote. *Texted. No response.*

They'd agreed to meet forty minutes earlier than the old man's seven o'clock, because what if the old man lied? What if there was no cure? What if he didn't show? Would they track him down? Kill him? Make him pay for their desperation in his hope? Pain twisted the thoughts in her ears.

The old man had been right about the president, about his being Pain-free. Everyone in the government was, from what she could tell. But what if he never intended to bring them enough for a cure? What if he intended only to let them try the one dose? What would they do? There was only one abandoned mine in the area she could think of, only one she'd discovered with Crow.

Hugo placed a martini in front of Lorelei and poured a shot of whiskey for himself. He left the nearly full bottle next to his glass, and he walked around the bar to take the seat next to Lorelei.

Lorelei's heart pounded as she wrote, *Did he jump????*

*We'll all jump, if this cure isn't real, but no, not Noah, not now, not with his daughter on her way. His granddaughter's life.*

*Maybe he went to find them.*

"Maybe," Hugo mouthed. He shrugged.

They both looked toward the door.

Lorelei picked up her martini and drank it down. The itch of a hundred bugs crawled deep in her ears. Crow whimpered, having not found Noah, and she picked him up to put him on her lap. She didn't hear his whimper – it was hard to hear anything but Speak Easy through Pain – but she knew his whimpering face. Hugo tipped his head at her empty glass. She nodded yes and he made her a second martini, but the drink had no more effect than the first.

It was nearly seven, almost time. Where was Noah?

Hugo opened his jacket to show Lorelei he'd tucked a scalpel into his inside pocket. Lorelei leaned over the bar and grabbed a knife that came within easy reach of her fingertips. An eight-inch blade. She laid it on the ledge under the bar meant for customers' handbags.

She held up a tiny camera she wore on a strap around her neck. A spy camera. It recorded sound. It recorded video. It was small. She used it often to record adventures with Crow. Hugo gave her a thumbs up. No smile.

7:10; 7:15; 7:30.

Hugo threw his arms around her, all the way around her. He held onto her. The clock ticked. He smelled warm. He smelled like Hugo. She thought he might cry.

"You stay here," she mouthed. Lorelei handed Crow to Hugo. *Something's wrong!* she wrote. *I am going to get us that cure. I know where it is, Hugo. It's the only mine in the area. It has to be it.* She grabbed a second piece of paper and drew a quick map. *Crow and I have been here a few times.*

"I'm going with you," mouthed Hugo.

"No… You… have… to… stay." *Noah might come back here. He might be hurt. He might need you. The old man might show.*

"Lorelei, no," mouthed Hugo. *You're blind out there. Pain won't let you hear.*

*It's still light out. I'll be fine. I'll be quick,* she wrote back. She took hold of his arm, just below his shoulder. "I… know… these… woods… It… ease… for… me… bet… er… for… me… a… lone… I… know… the… way… I… see… fine." She pointed to the camera around her neck.

***

Lorelei held the strap taut and the camera out in front of her, and she wound her way through the old miner's trail. But she wasn't herself. She tripped, and for a split second, Lorelei couldn't tell whether she fell up or down. She didn't hear leaves crunch. No branches snapped. If she hadn't put her hand on his leg to prop herself up, she would never have noticed the man. Her heart pounded in her head. Too loud. Her heart pounded too loud.

She looked through the camera lens to keep her eyes open. It was Jack, the old guy, the miner. His head was cocked to one side against a tree root. There was a bullet hole in his cheek. Four more bullet wounds, splats of blood on his white shirt, went into his chest and his abdomen. His eyes were open. Her own eyes tried to shut. Lorelei let the camera drop on its strap.

Her eyes twitched. Her hands went up to her face. Down. She forced them down. She could do this. She had to do this. "Jack… Jack." She shook his shoulders. She ran her fingers along the outside of his wrist. Nothing. No pulse. The Pain drilled in her ears. She reached into his shirt pockets. No packets, no vial, no pills. His pants pockets. Nothing. She rolled him to his left to check his back pocket. Nothing. To his right. A bag. She pulled out a tiny plastic bag filled with white powder. It looked like cocaine. Or heroine. Or fentanyl.

She lifted the camera over her head, and she laid it on the ground. She opened the bag and poured the contents in her palm. She picked up the camera and she pointed it at herself. She filmed herself licking the white powder from her hand. Ten seconds. Thirty seconds. The sticks in her ears were less sharp, the itch less frantic, the shrill high-pitched scream was faded. "Is it working?" she said aloud. She could hear her own voice. It was strong. It was clear. It was painless. "I can hear," she told the camera. "It works. I can hear."

Ten steps up the path, she found Noah. He was leaning against a tree. His eyes were closed. His shirt was soaked in blood.

Lorelei knelt beside him, and she lifted his shirt. She could feel his body trying to shut down. "Oh, Noah." Blood pumped from a hole in his abdomen, and she saw her brother.

Noah opened his eyes. Noah. Her safe Noah. She put her hand on his chest. The beat was soft. "You're gonna be fine, Noah. I'm gonna take care of you." He tried to smile.

She took off her jacket. She took the knife and her cap from its pockets, and she got her jacket behind Noah, around his middle. She pushed her cap onto the wound. She tied the arms of her jacket tightly over the cap. Noah struggled to breath, and she lifted his head.

Crow. He came out of nowhere.

"I knew you wouldn't let your old Noah die, Crow, not without seeing me one more time." His voice was faint. It was slow. It sounded like Speak Easy. Crow licked Noah's face. He laid his head on Noah's side.

"You're talking, Noah."

"It works, Leilei. I took it. The stuff works." She tried to smile. She watched him breathe.

"Did you kill Jack, Noah?"

"No. I begged him to take me with him." His words fought for air. "We were going to get full doses for everyone, Leilei. You, Anna, Hugo. It was the mayor. The mayor was behind the trees."

"The mayor?"

"The mayor shot us. We were so close, Leilei." Noah closed his eyes. She took hold of his face.

"Noah. Noah, don't."

"Leilei." His eyes opened. "Anna and Eva…"

"I'll take care of them, Noah. I'll get the stuff for us all. Don't worry about Anna and Eva." She lifted his shirt. Blood soaked the jacket she had tied around his wound.

"You're a good boy, Crow." Crow had crawled on top of Noah's chest, and he laid his hand on the dog. He stroked his head. "You're a good boy, Crow. You're a good boy. Be a good boy, Crow." He closed his eyes. His hand dropped.

Still lying on Noah's chest, Crow began a low rolling *errrr*. He growled louder. He barked. He licked Noah's face. He got down and poked at

Noah's hand with his nose. He sat still. Lorelei collapsed on the only father she knew.

The howl began low at first, almost talking, as if Crow was begging his friend to get up, and then he threw his head back to the heavens to cry. Raw. Soulful. Heart wrenching.

Lorelei grabbed her knife from the ground, and she turned it over in her hand. "Stay with me Crow," she said. Her eyes were open, wide open.

***

Lorelei and Crow stood at the end of the path, in the woods at the edge of the clearing, and she made sure her camera was on.

"I had to kill them, you idiot. What kind of guard are you?" It was the mayor. He was talking to a man in a security guard uniform who stood at the entrance to the mine. A newly installed iron gate blocked the opening. Two jeeps and four or five small trucks attached to cargo hoppers were parked across from where Lorelei stood, on the opposite side of the clearing. And she could see Hugo. Hugo was ducking and diving between the trucks. What did he think he was he doing?

"This mine is my ticket out of here, you idiot. You're supposed to be protecting my property."

"Your property?"

"Damn right."

"It's government property."

"I'm the mayor of this damn town. The government pays me for the rights to this mine. Found 'em a good baby collection center, too. Couple of caves down the road. Started construction already. Should bring me another several million at least. Now, give me those keys. You're too stupid to be holding them."

The mayor was pointing the gun at the guard and the guard threw the keys to the ground. "I quit," he said.

"Oh, no, you don't. You had yourself a little shootout here. We're going to go collect ourselves some bodies."

Lorelei grabbed Crow and ran into the woods, just as the two rode by in one of the small cargo trucks. The keys were still on the ground, and Lorelei made a dash for the clearing with Crow in her hand, grabbing the keys and running back into the woods. Hugo gave her a thumbs up from under a jeep, just as the mayor came back in the truck with the bodies of Noah and Jack.

"Help me pull them out of here," he told the guard, and they dragged Noah and Jack around the clearing. "There. No. Over there. That's perfect. Looks just like the three of you exchanged some gunfire. Like you were doing your due diligence protecting the merchandise. Let me see your gun for a minute." The guard handed him his gun and the mayor shot the guard in the chest. The guard dropped and the mayor put his gun on top of the guard. He laid the guard's gun next to Jack, making sure to get the proper fingerprints on each. "Perfect, looks like they stole your gun and a proper confrontation ensued. Not that the police in this stupid town will even try to figure it out. Now where are those keys?"

Lorelei could see Hugo making his way through the trucks to the guard's body. "No," she yelled out from the woods before the mayor turned to see Hugo. Hugo ducked, but Crow ran out and the mayor grabbed him. He held Crow by the neck with an outstretched arm, dangling Crow in the air out in front of him. He pointed a gun at the dog. "I'll kill him, Lorelei." Her heart raced.

She stepped out of the woods. "Not if you want your keys." She held up the keys. She stepped back into the woods. Hugo was sneaking up the side when the mayor turned and fired the gun. Hugo fell backward. He was on the ground. "He's not dead, Lorelei, but I'll kill them both. I'll kill them both and then I'll kill you." He moved to stand over Hugo, still dangling Crow by the neck.

"You won't find the keys if you kill me, Mayor." Lorelei was moving through the woods to behind the mayor.

"Which one first, Lorelei? Which one do you love more?" He cocked the gun. "This one?" He pointed the gun at Crow. "Or this one?" He pointed the gun at Hugo. "Eeny, meeny, miny, moe." He pointed the gun back and forth. Lorelei was behind him now, and she pulled out her knife and readied the blade in her hand. The mayor landed the gun at Crow's head.

Lorelei charged. The mayor turned. The mayor fired, again and again, but she kept on running. Every bit of her strength, her rage, her fear, driving the knife up into the man's underarm, the arm holding the gun, sinking part of its handle into the skin. He screamed as she fell on top of him to the ground. He was bleeding, spurting blood. Her brother's injury, pumping blood from the artery in his underarm. She pushed herself off him, away from the blood.

Her shoulder hurt. She had two bullet wounds to her shoulder. Hugo lay against a truck. The wound in his chest was on his right side and he struggled to get air in and out. She helped him to his feet, to inside a jeep. She went back to open the gate.

Inside, lights, like stars in the dark, lit a map, mine locations throughout the U.S., and she filmed it. Storage shelves filled with metal boxes lined the rock walls. She lifted a string of keys that hung from a hook, each marked with the letter of the alphabet. She opened an "A" box. Packets of white powder filled the box. She loaded four "A" boxes into the jeep. She went back and did it again. Voices. Voices were coming from inside the mine.

"Hugo… you… o… kay?"

"Okay."

The voices were closer.

She handed Hugo a packet of white powder. Crow sat between them in the jeep.

"Your… eyes… are… open," said Hugo.

Lorelei smiled. "Let's go." She knew how to get away in the woods.

### Part Five: There's No Place Like Home

Lorelei shook the pan on the stove as the popcorn popped, and she sighed. It was a sigh of release, a sigh of satisfaction. It came from an overwhelming appreciation of everything. She looked at Hugo on her sofa watching television. She looked at Crow sleeping next to him belly up. She gave herself time to take it all in, time to feel the tingling sensation of warmth that came from seeing them, from being there in that moment, from hearing all that was around her.

She sat on the other side of Crow and passed Hugo the bowl of popcorn. He kissed her.

"They're just about to start their sign off banter," he said. He was watching the *Evening News with Robbie and Kim*, Lorelei's old station. Robbie had helped Lorelei get her video out to sister stations across the United States.

"I saw the rocking giraffe and little green ark today, that Anna put out in front of Noah's. I'm glad she decided to take over the place."

"Shh," said Hugo, pointing to the television. "I want to listen. They're talking about you, again."

"How long has it been, Robbie, since we've been back on the air? A month?"

"A month, Kim."

"And we're still thanking Leilei and Crow every day." They each pointed to their ears.

"But today, we'd like to end the show on this happy note. As of today, Kansas State University's National Bio and Agro-Defense Facility, ground zero for the original virus, is officially closed. You folks in Kansas…"

"And the world."

"And the world, don't have to worry anymore."

"You know what, Robbie? That's where the president should serve his prison term, the president and the rest of his corrupt government."

"Maybe they will, Kim. Maybe, they will.

"Did you hear they're making a movie, Robbie?"

"I did, Kim. What do you think they'll call it?"

"Has to be *Leilei and Crow Save the World*, Robbie."

"It has to be."

## The Rumor That Refused to Die

### C.A. Verstraete

Amanda Hayes never expected her history teacher to talk about rumors in connection with a real newspaper story.

"Do you mean that story wasn't true?" she asked. "It says the policeman died in 1950 after his car fell into a giant sinkhole. I thought newspapers had to print the truth?"

"You be the judge," her teacher said. "People still say the whole story wasn't told. For your homework, due next Friday, I want you to write about how the facts of a historic event can get changed over time. I'm also requiring you to research like it used to be done, before computers. I'll be expecting a list with the microfilm, newspaper and book sources you use. You must use at least one of each."

Amanda joined her classmates in a collective groan.

"What do you think?" Amanda asked her best friend Katie as they walked home after school. "Do you think it's true or fake?"

Katie shrugged. "It sounds strange, but I heard on TV about a whole house falling into a giant sinkhole. I guess it can happen."

"Not too often, I hope. See you tomorrow."

She went inside, put her backpack on the table, and followed the scent of fried chicken to the kitchen.

"Mmm, my favorite! Mom, do you know what happened to that policeman who died in 1950? I heard something was underneath the street and—"

Her mother laughed and shook her head. "And nothing. Honey, every time they talk about that story in school, the urban legends start. I heard those stories when I was a girl."

"But they sound so real."

"Rumors often do," her mother explained. "Everyone back then was afraid of nuclear war and being attacked by the Russians. Remember those old monster and giant creature movies we used to watch on Saturday night? They played on people's fears. Same here. The poor man died in a terrible accident. That's all there is to it. Alright?"

Amanda shrugged. "Sure."

Except she wasn't.

She knew her mother wouldn't lie to her, but it seemed odd hearing the same rumors decades later. Why? Amanda remained convinced that something was missing, but what? She vowed to find some answers and write about it for her class paper.

***

Her search at the library that weekend turned up nothing new. The newspaper office didn't have any records other than the same stories her teacher shared about the accident and funeral. Even the police department couldn't offer anything beyond the commemorative plaque hanging in the lobby.

Back home, Amanda paced across her bedroom, wondering what she was missing. "Don't you think it's weird, Katie?"

Her best friend looked up from the book open in front of her and shrugged. "You like weird, but it's due Friday, you know. You don't have enough time to go too deep into this."

"I know, but I can't stop thinking something's wrong." Amanda sighed as she slid a pen across the scarred surface of her desk. "Such a big event and years later, you still hear some weird rumor, and there's hardly any information on it. Doesn't that seem strange?"

"If you say so. What'll be strange is what you tell our teacher about your assignment not being done."

"I'll finish it, but I have an idea… will you help me?"

Her friend stopped writing and rolled her eyes. "I don't like the sound of that. Help you with what?"

"Something easy. You like history. Let's go back to the library tomorrow. You can help me look up the newspaper microfilms a few days before the accident. Maybe something else happened that everyone's overlooked. I bet nobody looked at the earlier records."

"Hmm, that's possible, but I have to get my paper done, too."

"You'll finish, I know you. How about I bribe you with ice cream sundaes?"

"Okay, that sounds like a plan. Can we start now? I'll take strawberry, with lots of whipped cream."

Amanda smiled. "Strawberry it is. We better hurry before my mom gets home. You know she won't like us eating ice cream before dinner."

***

The next afternoon, Amanda clutched the folder containing copies of the stories she'd found, glad they'd spent the time reading the old reels of microfilmed newspapers.

"Can you believe it?" she asked Katie as they walked home. "It's amazing we found this! I bet no one else took the time to look up any of this stuff before the policeman died, at least not five days before."

She pulled out the paper again and began to read: "Listen to this: 'WORM ATTACK? August 13, 1950, by Sarah Spencer—A seventy-eight-year-old man was taken to Sandersville Hospital after being 'attacked' by an unknown creature while he was working on the sump pump in his basement. He said it looked like a reddish-colored snake or a worm. 'The thing came out of the pit,' he said. 'It was as thick as my thigh, and around 20-feet long or so. It lunged at me, scared me half to death.'"

Katie snorted. "C'mon, a giant worm? That really can't be true. Why would a newspaper even print that?"

"I don't know, but it's proof there's more to this than everyone's said. We'll have to go back and do another search, see what else we find. I'll ask the librarian if she knows about any other resources. There has to be something, right?"

Katie let out a long sigh. "I guess. I have to get another book for my paper anyway. I'll expect an extra big strawberry sundae when we're done."

"You got it, with tons of whipped cream and double cherries, too. Thanks, Katie."

"Yeah, yeah. I wish you didn't get such big ideas. I'm writing about the story and the obsession back then with Martians and spaceships to show how some stories weren't true. There's way more information to find on that. Spending all my time in the library isn't what I'd call fun."

***

The next day's search turned up something completely unexpected when the librarian called Amanda to the desk.

"I found this folder on one of the shelves in the archives," the librarian said. "I'll let you check it out if you promise to be careful and bring it back by the weekend."

Amanda tried to hold in her excitement. "I'll be careful, I promise, thank you!"

Once home, she rushed Katie upstairs so they could examine the contents before dinner.

"Wow, look at this! There are all kinds of

newspaper clippings and some kind of scrapbook in here." She pulled out the thin booklet and opened it. "It says, 'Property of S. Spencer'. That has to be the reporter who wrote the story Mrs. Thompson read in class. I think we'll find something here for sure!"

"Mandy, I can't believe I'm saying this, but... I guess you were right. I'll call my mom and see if I can stay for dinner."

"Good idea."

She waited for Katie to finish her call before grabbing one of the aged papers with care. The musty smell made her sneeze.

"Here's the first story: 'POLICE MOURN DEATH OF OFFICER. August 18, 1950: The city has declared a day of mourning following the death of five-year Sandersville Police Officer Dwayne Roberts, who was killed after his car fell into a giant sinkhole that opened on Main Street.

"'"This was a horrific tragedy," said Police Chief Dan Johnson. "We lost a good man from our ranks. State, local and federal law enforcement and fire officials are assisting in the investigations."'"

She stopped reading. "That's odd," Amanda said. "It seems like a lot of police and government being involved for only an accident, doesn't it?"

"Does that mean there's more they're not saying?" Katie asked.

"Could be." She scanned the story again. "Whoa, listen to this: 'One witness, who wanted to remain anonymous, said she saw what looked like a giant worm reach out of the hole and swallow the car.' That's all it says."

"A worm, again? Really?" Katie asked. "And an anonymous witness."

"Yeah… what if that witness wasn't real?" Amanda asked. She looked up from the notebook as her mother called from downstairs.

"Amanda? I'm home. Dinner'll be quick tonight, chicken patties, ten minutes."

"Okay, I'll be right down. Katie's here, too."

"That's fine, I have plenty. Come set the table."

The two of them clopped down the stairs, with Amanda babbling excitedly as she took out the plates and told her friend to get the silverware.

"Mom, you'll never believe it! The librarian gave me this folder from the archives. It has newspaper stories by that lady who wrote about the policeman's death. And one mentions the giant worm in the street. It really was in the newspaper!"

Her mother paused in dishing out the salad. "Huh, I'm surprised the library had that. What I didn't tell you, and you probably won't find in there, is that the reporter Miss Spencer had some kind of breakdown. She was in the psychiatric ward in what they used to call the mental hospital for a while. That's really why she retired. She was an award-winning reporter and editor before that. Your grandmother told me everyone felt sorry for her having such a public collapse. She's still a recluse."

Amanda stopped eating and glanced over at Katie. "Still? You… you mean she's alive?"

"Wow, she must be ancient," Katie whispered.

"Girls, please. Be respectful. I'd say she must be in her nineties now. She still lives in the same house here in town."

"That means I can talk to her. Maybe she'll tell me what really happened!"

"Honey, listen to me," her mother said. "I want you to be careful. We don't know if she's well, or how fragile she might be. You shouldn't upset her. If she doesn't want to talk, you have to leave her alone. Clean up and then time for homework. Katie, do you need a ride?"

A beep sounded outside.

"No, thanks, Mrs. Hayes," Katie said. "That's my dad. Mandy, see you tomorrow."

"'Night, Katie, thanks."

After clearing the table, Amanda grabbed her mother's phone and looked up the name. "Mom, I found the number. Can I call her?"

Her mother glanced at the clock on the wall. "Well, it's only five. You can try, but I don't want you to be a pest if she doesn't answer."

"Thanks, Mom. I'll be in my room."

Amanda ran upstairs and grabbed her own phone off the bed. Her fingers shook slightly as she punched in the number. She waited, and after several rings, a shaky voice answered.

"Hello, Miss Spencer? Hi, I'm Amanda Hayes. I'm working on a paper for school and I thought you could help. I found a scrapbook at the library with some old stories you wrote in 1950. I just wanted to ask—it won't take—Oh, okay, I'm sorry."

Amanda sighed in disappointment as she ended the call. She punched in her friend's number.

"Hey, Katie. I just called Sarah Spencer. No, she hung up on me. She said that was a long time ago and she had nothing more to say. Yeah, see you tomorrow."

She pondered her friend's advice to keep looking. "I can't give up that easy," Amanda muttered. "There's more to this. I just have to find out what and get Miss Spencer to talk to me."

Paging through the scrapbook, Amanda found a letter from the president of the American Society for the Prevention of Cruelty and Harm to Animals (ASPCHA). It read, "August 19, 1950, Dear Editor, we at the ASPCHA protest any potential action planned against a creature of the earth. Harming this creature before it can be caught and set free in a safer environment is against all precepts of humanity and violates our explicit vow to protect all forms of wildlife, whether they be above or below ground. We at the society will do whatever it takes to ensure this animal comes to no harm. We ask that this letter be published in your next issue."

Amanda searched the other pages in the scrapbook but couldn't find any other mention of the letter's contents.

The next story she found dated August 20 quoted Police Chief Dan Johnson as saying, "I'm not going to waste time debating about some supposed underground monster when one of my men died in a tragic accident. People need to quit watching those fake creature movies and face real life."

Amanda wondered: did that mean the letter, which would've proven that someone else had known about the worm, had never been published? Had it been purposefully withheld? She sighed. The more she read, the more complicated this story became. Now she had even more questions than when she'd started.

The next story she found added an even more bizarre twist. She read, "August 21, 1950, RAVAGED BODY FOUND AT CHEMICAL PLANT. A night worker at the Avion Chemical Plant on Sheridan Road reported finding a badly mangled body in the company's back lot Saturday night.'"

The next story was dated August 28 with the headline, 'CHEMICAL PLANT SHUT DOWN.'

Another brief story said two people had gone to the hospital for some kind of bites. Why in the world did that reporter save all these stories?

On a whim, she punched in her friend's phone number again. "Hey, Katie, listen to this. I found a small story talking about people being bit by something. Another story says the government was investigating this plant for producing a banned chemical. I wonder... do you think all this is connected somehow?"

She had to laugh at Katie's question about the giant radioactive bugs in those old scary movies. "Okay, okay, I know, it sounds ridiculous, right? See you tomorrow."

After ending the call, Amanda decided to talk to a couple of the older neighbors she'd helped with errands. Maybe they'd remember something about the original incident.

Her next-door neighbor Mrs. Miller snorted and laughed outright, telling her the newspaper "made a mockery of that young man's death. It's baloney. They shoulda been ashamed of themselves. It was a disgrace."

Another neighbor, Mr. Jones, said much the same.

Amanda didn't get it. It made no sense. She vowed to keep digging.

***

Further searches in other local history books came to nothing. Amanda had hoped to find a solution for her paper, but she'd ended up empty-handed. Now time had run out.

"I hope our teacher thinks this is okay," she told Katie as they handed their papers in. "All I could do was write about the stuff I looked up, the couple odd stories I found, the questions I have, and how it's still a mystery. I feel like it's unfinished."

"You did your best," Katie said. "I think Mrs. Thompson will understand. Actually, you found some things in that scrapbook no one knew about. I think she'll give you a good mark for your research."

***

Amanda smiled as she admired the big red A marked on both hers and Katie's papers the next afternoon.

"Whew, I'm glad that's done with. Want to come over? I'm going to go through the scrapbook one more time before I return it."

Once home, they went to her room and dug through the booklet's final clippings, disappointed to find nothing else.

"Well, I guess that's it," Amanda said. "I'll take it back to the library tomorrow." She almost closed the book but spotted something sticking out from the back lining. "Hey, what's this?"

She unfolded a yellowed piece of paper with two small clippings glued onto it. "Listen to this, 'August 29, 1950, STRANGE INSECTS FOUND IN LOCAL GARDENS. The health department has investigated reports of people finding clusters of unusual tiny red worms in their gardens. Health Department Director Mabel Williams said that the insects appear to be harmless but warn that people shouldn't touch them.'"

"Did they really have some kind of worm outbreak?" Katie asked.

Amanda shrugged and continued reading. "The second story is dated August 30, 1950. 'REPORTER BITTEN BY INSECTS. Staff reporter Sarah Spencer is expected to make a full recovery after she was bitten by what she says were tiny worms hiding in her newspaper Tuesday.'

"'Spencer said, 'I thought it was a spider. I felt something bite me and managed to dial the operator before I passed out.' Talk about weird! Why would worms, and not ants or some other bugs, be in her paper?"

"Since when do worms bite?" Katie asked and shivered.

The trill of the phone and her mother's call from downstairs interrupted their musing. "Honey? It's for you."

Amanda ran down and took the phone her mother held out with a whispered warning. "It's Miss Spencer. Remember what I said."

Amanda nodded and took the phone. 'Hi, Miss Spencer... What...? Sure, I can be there, thank you."

"Mom, she wants me to come to her house at six. Can I go?"

"You should've asked first, but very well. I'll drive you and wait outside. We can take Katie home when you're done."

After dinner, Amanda's mother parked the car in front of the elderly woman's tidy lemon-colored bungalow, the front garden beds filled with rows of bright red and yellow tulips.

"I wish you could come in with me, Katie, but Miss Spencer said she didn't want any other visitors," Amanda explained. "She was pretty insistent about that. Even kind of cranky. I didn't want to get her mad and have her say no."

"Mandy, that's all right. I understand. At least she let you come over. You can tell me what happened when you come out."

Amanda walked down the sidewalk and stopped at the front of the house, admiring all the flowers. She peeked through the screen door, surprised to find the inner door open.

"Hello? Miss Spencer, it's Amanda Hayes." Getting no answer, she hesitated a moment before going inside. "Miss Spencer?"

A raspy voice came from the other end of the house. "In here, girl. I'm in the living room."

Amanda went through the kitchen, down the hall, and past the cellar to the dim living room where an old woman sat in a floral armchair. "Hi, I'm…"

"I heard you," the woman said, her voice frosty. "I'm old, not deaf. Now sit. Tell me what you want."

"Um…" Amanda gulped nervously and bit her lip. "I was doing a paper for school on that policeman's death in 1950. Well, I finished it, I got an A." She paused and then rushed on under the woman's surly glare. "Uh, I still had a few questions about… about the accident…"

Miss Spencer jerked her head slightly and coughed. Amanda waited for some kind of response as the woman continued to fidget.

"Well, what of it?" Miss Spencer asked. "I told you, there's nothing more to say."

Amanda frowned, questioning why the old woman had invited her over if she didn't want to talk.

She watched in fascination as the woman's face twitched, the deep wrinkles quivering like tremors during an earthquake. *She sure is the nervous type,* Amanda thought. Maybe those rumors were right.

She plunged on. "I found the story you wrote, the one where a witness said she saw a giant worm swallow the car. Um, there wasn't a witness, was there?"

"You calling me a liar, girl? Where'd you get that, did you steal it?" the old woman hissed.

"No, I didn't!" Amanda jumped back in shock when the old woman swiped at her with dagger-like fingernails.

"That story was only in one place, my scrapbook the library stole from me," the old lady accused. "They STOLE it. Borrowed it and never gave it back. They're the ones who told everyone I was sick… *Crazy,* some of them said. Forced me to retire. Now some snot-nosed whippersnapper questions me? How dare you!"

Stunned by Miss Spencer's angry outburst, Amanda didn't know what to do. Should she stay or leave? A minute later, the woman groaned, her face crinkling in pain.

"Miss Spencer, are you alright? Should I call an ambulance?"

The old woman shook her head. "No, no…" She growled deep in her throat. "I missed lunch. You… you better go." A scowl distorted her face, making the deep furrows in her cheeks tremble.

"Miss Spencer?"

The former reporter glared, her eyes narrowed like slits. "Go, I said, GO!"

Amanda stumbled over her own feet as the old lady stood on shaky legs and shuffled forward, her steps jerky.

*She's not well,* Amanda thought, as the woman moaned again and smacked her lips like a fish out of water.

The senior's strange behavior continued, with Amanda making sure she stayed out of reach of those hideously long claws. Still, she couldn't leave. Not yet.

She had to know what was going on. Something was dreadfully wrong here. Something…

"Mandy, look out!" Katie yelled from the hall.

Amanda turned, surprised to see her friend standing there. She scooted out of reach just in time when Miss Spencer swiped at her again. The girl grimaced as the old woman's mouth opened wide.

Amanda gasped and watched the hideous scene before her in shock. Miss Spencer's mouth opened wider and wider. Something red and slimy moved there. Seconds later, a giant worm slithered past the old woman's lips. Slime dripped down her chin.

"Eww! Katie, watch out!"

"Mandy, oh, ick, run, RUN!"

The girls scurried backward, trying to put some distance between themselves and *it*. The creature rose higher and higher, more of its ugly, ridged body emerging from the old crone's mouth, even as her withered body wobbled to hold its weight.

Amanda knew they had to get out of there, but she didn't want to leave this *thing* here to attack anyone else. She saw the large push broom next to the open cellar door and got an idea. Grabbing it, she stabbed at the worm with the broom's thick bristled head and leapt aside as the creature quickly lowered itself to her level. It quivered and moved closer, its gaping mouth revealing row after row of tiny, dagger-like teeth.

Amanda thrust the broom again at the old lady's weakened body. The worm chomped its ugly teeth while it swayed from side to side. Finally, the monster shuddered as its host thumped to the floor, the old lady's near-useless arms grabbing weakly at the open doorway.

"Quick, Katie, help me!"

The two of them shoved the broom at the now still form. The worm flailed and tried to twist itself out of reach. It stretched further away from them, its mouth still snapping like an alligator's.

"Now!" Amanda yelled. "Push, Katie! Push as hard as you can!"

They leaned on the broom with all their weight. "PUUSH!" Amanda yelled.

The worm and the old woman's body slid past the open doorway and dropped into the dirt cellar with a loud thump.

"Whew, it's dead."

"Wow, oh, wow, I never, ever thought I'd see something like that," Katie said. "I don't think I'll sleep tonight."

"Me, either. Want to stay over?"

"Only if we can have strawberry sundaes again," Katie said.

"Deal!" Amanda answered.

A voice behind them broke up their conversation. "Amanda, I got tired of waiting outside. What…?" Her mother looked down into the cellar with a grimace. "Ugh, is that what I think it is?"

Amanda nodded.

"Unbelievable," her mother muttered. "I'd heard

some talk about Miss Spencer being infected after those worms bit her. Who'd have thought it was true? You girls go out to the car. I'll call the police."

***

Amanda wasn't at all surprised to see the story in the next day's newspaper calling Miss Spencer's death a tragic accident from a fall at home.

"You think they know what really happened?" Amanda asked her friend.

Katie shrugged. "Maybe, maybe not, but who would believe it? Would you?"

"No, not if I hadn't seen it with my own eyes, and I'm sorry I did."

"Me too, and I'm not telling anyone. Ever. I'd rather forget about it."

"You and me both," Amanda said. "I'll let it be another mystery someone else can uncover."

"Yeah, in like a hundred years," Katie added. "I think you should leave the mysteries to the experts."

"You bet. From now on, I'm letting Nancy Drew do the solving in her books. C'mon, let's go make some sundaes."

"Best thing you ever said," Katie answered. "Make mine strawberry—this time with chocolate sauce."

"Good choice," Amanda said. "Change can be good."

They looked at each other and laughed.

## The Evil Eye

## Carlton Herzog

Look at your body
A painted puppet, a poor toy
Of jointed parts ready to collapse,
A diseased and suffering thing
With a head full of false imaginings.
--*The Dhammapada*

The eradication of humanity did not come on the heels of prophecy. Nor were there attendant signs and wonders. No comets thundered across the heavens, no banshees wailed, no seers cried "The end is nigh." Instead, it arrived in Brooklyn amid the frantic rattle of the cicadas and the scent of freshly mowed summer grass. It announced itself with the whirring blades of the Yard Beast Ten Thousand when two arborists voluntarily plunged headfirst into the Beast's rapacious maw. One shaken eyewitness described the joint suicide with the sangfroid of a sports commentator: "It all happened so fast. One minute they were feeding trees into the mulcher. The next I saw a pair of feet leave the ground. Then feet and legs twisting in the hopper like helicopter blades. When the body got stuck, the second guy jerked the legs this way and that way to keep things moving. Once the jam had been cleared, he watched until the last of his partner shot out the exhaust in a sparkling red mist. Then he jumped into the shredder himself. Say what you will, it was a fine example of teamwork."

When the two tree cutters took their leap, I was home on my lunch break. There was no reason for me, a homicide detective, to be called to that suicide scene. But before the Yard Beast's crimson spray was cold, I was called to a murder suicide on the next street over. Five workers on a road resurfacing project had laid down in the hot asphalt and were crushed to death by a slow-moving steamroller. The victim's blood flattened faces looked like comical Halloween pies.

I asked the driver, "Does human life mean nothing to you?"

He smiled and said, "Haven't you heard? The ideal population size is zero. Besides, they pleaded with me to do it. I wanted to join them, but the roller doesn't have an autopilot. So, I had to operate the controls."

I sensed no innate depravity in the man. Just a gaping hole where a soul ought to have been. I pictured myself throwing a coin into a void expecting the ping of it hitting bottom but hearing nothing, so deep was the abyss into which it had fallen. Whatever humanity the fellow had entered the world with at birth had been stripped away. And I suspected, the same was true of those poor devils we were excavating from the newly paved road. For myself, I wanted to know who or what had compelled them to drink the Kool-Aid or whatever else it was that produced such self-destructive behavior

***

Things only got worse from there. One day later, and four blocks away, I, together with uniformed officers, executed a warrant on a modest two-story colonial. Earlier, the occupant's sister had come to visit. She found her blood-smeared sibling drinking blood from her own artery. By dint of an extraordinary effort, the woman had digested the skin and muscle of her right arm down to the bone. The appalled sister applied a rough tourniquet and rushed her to the emergency room. Enroute to the hospital, the self-cannibalizing woman admitted that she had cut off her husband's head and tossed it into a bucket. She further admitted that she then played with the cadaver for "two to three hours" after his death, using several knives to dismember the body. She told her sister that a bread knife worked "the best," because of the "serrated blade."

We found the husband's malodorous remains in the living room. As a procedural matter, we searched the rest of the house for evidence. There were decomposing bodies and empty anti-freeze jugs in every room of the house. In the garage, we found a large "quilt" composed of heads, limbs, and torsos spread out on the garage floor. The remains had been joined in three layers like fabric. There was a mechanical sewing machine and specialized long-armed quilting device adjacent to a butcher block. Meat hooks strung along the wall held limbs and torsos for future quilting projects. Yet, the most disturbing aspect of the gruesome scene was the tome made from human skin titled *The Book of the Disquiet*. It contained suicide contracts wherein the party of the first part agreed that in exchange for a lethal anti-freeze cocktail, the party of the second part could do with their remains as she pleased. Thus, we had encountered another instance of a mass suicide. But I was no closer to understanding this irresistible urge toward self-extinction.

***

The next day, my partner, Sage Gallo, and I visited the medical examiner. While we waited to see the doctor, I found myself staring at a lithograph of Hans Holbein the Younger's 1533 *The Ambassadors*. The image contained a huge, distorted skull that appeared like an indiscriminate slash across the canvass. But when viewed from an angle, it revealed itself in three-dimensions. It's one of the most famous uses of anamorphosis to communicate the impermanence of human endeavors and the decay that is inevitable with the passage of time.

"We've got ourselves a movable Theater of the Grotesque. A rash of murder and suicide within a four-block radius. But nothing seems to connect any of the players beyond a morbid psychology," I said.

Sage pointed to the lithograph and said, "We need to change our angle if we want to see the skull. Maybe this is a case of thought contagion. Like a software virus traveling on the Internet or a flu strain passing through a city, thought contagions proliferate by programming for their own propagation. Certain beliefs spread like viruses and evolve like microbes, as mutant strains vie for more adherents and more hosts. Just as people accumulate ideas, ideas accumulate people."

I smirked. His pedantic airs seemed absurd given his Hollywood attire. He wore a vintage Columbo raincoat and gangster fedora. It was deliberate sartorial boldness designed to get tongues wagging from the start, if only to express surprise or derision at his stylistic choices. Then there was his pronounced overbite. In the twenty first century, the orthodontically challenged should be a rare breed. Cosmetic dentistry was cheap, easy, and painless. Yet here was a man who insisted on looking as if he could eat apples through a fence.

I tried to keep a straight face as he droned on about mass sociogenic illness.

"History abounds with examples of collective insanity that burst on the scene then dissipate. In 1784, a nun who lived in a German convent began to bite her companions. The behavior soon spread through other convents in Germany, Holland, and Italy. In 1844, a nun who lived in a French convent inexplicably began to meow like a cat. Shortly thereafter, the other nuns in the convent began to meow as well. Eventually, all the nuns in the convent would meow together for a certain period, leaving the surrounding community astonished.

In 1971, 70,000 people at Fatima Spain claimed the sun zoomed toward Earth in a zigzag motion. Or consider the Heaven's Gate wackos. They were a religious sect founded by Marshall Applegate that combined apocalyptic Christian beliefs and UFO themes. The followers believed that they could transform into immortal beings. By rejecting their human nature, they could ascend to heaven and achieve the next evolutionary level. On March 26, 1997, police discovered 39 members of Heaven's Gate cult had committed mass suicide."

At the word mass suicide, I felt the need to retort. "Those examples have a demonstrated religious connection, whereas our cases are just random episodes of coincidental wacky behavior."

"Well, maybe the autopsy report will shed some light on things," Sage added.

Dr. Julian Frost, the medical examiner, did exactly that, but in the process raised more questions than he answered.

"Have you boys ever heard of cat scratch fever?"

"It's the thing that makes rats attracted to cat piss."

"The 'thing' as you so eloquently called it is a protozoan parasite called Toxoplasma. It can only reproduce in the gut of a cat. It comes out in cat feces which is then eaten by rodents. To reproduce, the parasite needs to get back into a cat. So, it manufactures cysts in the rat's brain that destroy the fear and anxiety circuits and amplify the sexual reward system with increased dopamine production. In short, when a rat is exposed to cat pheromones, its testes get bigger, not smaller."

"Okay, what do horny rats, and cats have to do with human murders and suicides?"

"The bodies of the deceased all had enlarged testes, ridiculous amounts of dopamine levels, and no shortage of encapsulated cysts in the brain."

"Great, they all had cat scratch fever."

"Alas, they did not. Despite the inflammatory and neurochemical markers, there was no sign of the parasite. Whatever made those suicides get sexually aroused in anticipation of taking their own lives is a mystery to me. But I can speculate. Government researchers, for example, have linked the low-frequency and mid-frequency sonar used by military ships, such as those operated by the U.S. Navy, to several mass strandings as well as other deaths and serious injuries among whales and dolphins. Military sonar sends out intense underwater sonic waves, essentially a very loud sound that can retain its power across hundreds of miles. Many beached whales in strandings associated with sonar also show evidence of physical injuries, including bleeding in their brains, ears, and internal tissues."

I snickered: "Are you suggesting that our perps and victims have been affected by sound waves?"

"It could be sound or something else. For example, research has shown that there are many ways that electromagnetic fields can be hazardous to human health, including **altering hormones or**

**behavior**, disabling internal organs like brain cells or reproductive systems, and inducing cancerous changes on DNA strands. That would be consistent with the cysts I found. The geographic proximity of the subjects to one another indicates a common transmission source."

Sage said, "I get that the brain and its satellite glands are susceptible to EM disruption. But this phenomenon seems a little too focused. It is redolent of Freud's death instinct—the force that makes living creatures strive for an inorganic state. How does extra radiation do that?"

Dr. Julian said, "At this juncture, I can only characterize what we are seeing as an imp of the perverse: a paradoxical urging toward wrong or self-destructive acts."

***

We spent the next few days chasing our tails. Then we received a tip. One Cedric Hardman, patient extraordinaire at the Mid-Town Manhattan Psychiatric Hospital, claimed to have foreseen the deaths we were investigating. I thought it was bullshit, but Sage, always on the look-out for human oddities, pressed me into joining him in the interview. Cedric went by the *nom du lunatique* of The Kraken. Although he sported no tentacles, he did have a prominent head with a beaklike nose suggesting an ancestry not altogether human. His psychosis, which had bred a demented grandeur of atrocious proportions, did nothing to mitigate his otherworldly aura.

"All hope abandon, ye who enter here. Welcome to my shining sanctuary where I will regale you with my not so pleasant prophecies. Lesson the first: the story you find yourselves in is but the prologue to the main narrative. A killing here, a suicide there with no discernible topography defined as it were by unseen meridians. Lesson the second: what began as isolated instances will soon proliferate like malignant cancer cells in the body."

"This nut is just wasting our time. I have places to be and things to do," I growled.

"I take it you don't find my egotistical magnificence very interesting. Fair enough, the metaphysical economy of my universe is not for everyone. But since you want some tidbit with meat on it, then know you will get it tonight. Next door and in your home."

"What do you mean?" I asked.

"You'll see. And when you come back, as I know you will, I suspect you will be more open-minded about the things I have to show you."

"Why not now?"

"Your pump needs to be primed for my fantastic tale. Now off with the both of you. I have nothing more to say."

***

When we left the Institute, Sage and I went our separate ways. He to a dive bar, me to my wife and three kids. Lasagna, a beer or two, and some "How was your day dear" talk was just the thing I needed to decompress. But as I turned onto my street, I found several squad cars and an ambulance parked in front of my neighbor's house. Curious, I walked over and spoke to one of the officers.

"So, what's the 411 Dave?"

"From what we can tell, your neighbor slit his wife and kid's throat and then his own. No note. There was no reason for it. They were happily married, financially secure, and otherwise model citizens. Makes no sense at all."

"For what it's worth there's been a lot of 'makes no sense' suicides going on today. Maybe it's something in the air."

"Or the times. People are crazier than they used to be."

The prospect of pleasant table talk gave way to hopeless cynicism as I walked across the lawn to my own house. Despite the gloomy atmospherics, or perhaps because of them, I wondered why my wife was not standing with the neighborhood gawkers at the curb.

"Marci, I'm home. Marci?"

I had not gone ten feet into the house when I saw my wife and three kids hanging by the neck from the second-floor banister. With their repulsively bloated and saggy bodies, and swollen puffy-lipped purple faces, they looked like corpses just dragged from a river and hung like rancid meat in a ghoul's back room.

I called 911, then I called Sage. When he got there, he brought me outside and sat me down on my porch.

"You'll stay with me tonight."

"That nutcase predicted this. How could he know? We need to get the truth out of him."

"Tomorrow. For now, give your statement to these officers, and then we'll hit the road. I've got an old hide-a-bed and plenty of liquor."

I did as he asked. But I could not sleep. I just stared at the clock, waiting for morning.

***

When we entered the interview room, Cedric gave us a broad smile.

"I see my prophecy came true. Otherwise, you would not be here."

"How did you know?"

As I looked into his black, depthless eyes, he said, "I exist in a realm that crossbreeds your mean streets reality with other dimensions of time and space. A phantasmagorical transcendence of limits if you will. But such transmutations are not for pedestrian minds. So, it is only grudgingly I show you the truth you seek but will not, in all likelihood, understand."

In that moment, I saw a projection on the wall. It was a laboratory of some sort with a testing room separated by a glass partition. On one side were two stylishly dressed young women in a room filled with axes, knives, maces, and swords. On the other, four experimenters in lab coats and a civilian wearing a red velvet cape and holding a wolf's head cane.

The female subjects sat contently waiting for instructions. Dr. Peter Zapffe, the lead experimenter, spoke to his lab assistants and his flamboyant visitor. He outlined the parameters of the experiment as follows:

"We call this the Evil Eye Protocol. Consider that the eyes are the doors of perception and the gateway to the soul. Many cultures already know that looks can kill. In Arabic it is called *al-ayn* (the eye). In Spanish it is *Mal de Ojo*. In India they say *Drishti*. In Ethiopia it is called the *Buda* and in Pakistan it is the *Nazar*. Plutarch the Greek philosopher believed that an evil eye gave off lethal invisible rays.

"Consistent with those beliefs, our current research shows a strong relationship between a person's eyes and the amygdala's fight or flight response. When two pairs of eyes meet, there is an exchange of information below the threshold of consciousness. I believe we can tap into that subliminal communications network to enter specific behavioral commands. To that end, my telepath Mr. Garibaldi will plant a command in the mind of subject number one to kill subject number two. Having already tested the efficacy of Mr. Garibaldi's mental manipulation skills, we know that subject number one will do as instructed. What we need to know is whether subject number one's gaze will simultaneously transmit the kill command to subject number two, such that subject two becomes equally homicidal. If today's optical experiment proves successful, then we can field test larger groups to understand the extent to which one telepathically infected person can create an optical chain reaction."

"The ineluctable modality of the visible," said the red-caped man known as Phillip Mainlander.

"Excuse me?"

"I forgot that you mad scientists tend to be philistines. I was quoting from James Joyce's *Ulysses*. The phrase means the sense of sight provides an unavoidable way of knowing reality, the knowledge provided being a kind of thought through the eyes."

"Mr. Mainlander, this is a weapons development facility funded by the American government. If one is going to do lethal experiments on human beings to create an outbreak of mass murder among an enemy population, it pays to be both a philistine and a lout. No one here has the soul of a poet, and I daresay, no one wants such a thing."

"Of that I have no doubt. Please proceed with your blood sport. Let us see if your baby science can elicit the primordial beast in these two guinea pigs."

When Garibaldi projected his thoughts into Subject One, she sprang to her feet and grabbed a hatchet. Subject Two stared wide-eyed but remained frozen. Subject One drove the hatchet into Subject Two's forehead, yanked it back out, then went for neck. The strike to the carotid artery sent a geyser into Subject One's face. Number One kept at it until Garibaldi gave her a sleep command, after which she slumped to the floor.

"I must admit this is very disappointing," a frustrated Zappfe said.

"Why not try again?"

"This is the fourth attempt, and I have not had so much as a glimmer of success. I am at my wits end."

"Then it's fortunate your employer, David Benatar, hired me on as a consultant."

"Are you a scientist?"

"In a manner of speaking."

"Either you are or you are not?"

"I am a mystic; where you stand upon the shore and see only the ocean's breakers, I see to the ocean floor. A benefit of having alliances with other orders of existence. Places where mirrors scream and the sky rains daggers."

"I want to throw you out on your ear for wasting my time, but I feel considerable admiration for your ability to cajole my boss into believing your mumbo-jumbo."

"Cajole is too mild a term. It was more enchantment than anything else. I used the very mechanisms you are trying to develop, namely, the transmission of will by gaze alone. You see, Dr. Zappfe, my interests dovetail with yours. Your success is my success."

"So, you're not kidding about the magic?"

"What you call magic is simply a higher order of science that relies on mystical configurations and apparatus sewn into the fabric of reality by the Great Maker. If one knows the right formula, then unlocking that science for personal use is no more difficult than combining hydrogen and oxygen to make water."

"So, what do you suggest?"

"You have the right idea of weaponizing the human gaze into a lethal glare. But you simply lack the power to make it so. I am offering you that power. Once your telepath's abilities are married to my dark magic, you can send your evil eyes out into the world and exterminate whomever you please with nothing more than a contagious glance."

"What does the magic do exactly?" asked Zappfe.

"It removes the fabulous illusions your kind employs to avoid seeing the truth of its situation. Much like the little Dutch boy pulling his finger from the dike. Once the anchoring belief systems and social distractions are removed, people must confront the nightmare of their ephemeral, suffering plagued existence. All their suppressed misanthropic tendencies will be unleashed, and their world will truly be hell where they are on the one hand the tormented souls and on the other the devils in it. They have no choice but to kill themselves or kill others *en masse.* Thus, you will rid yourselves of all your enemies without firing a shot."

The image faded. Sage gave me a look and asked, "Exactly how did you do that?"

"I don't know how, and I don't know why. The same can be said for those times I took my victims to abandoned buildings and accommodating sewers. Maybe I'm some demi-demon from some outré hell.

But if you ask the staff here, I am nothing more than a schizophrenic, who hears non-existent voices and sees non-existent things," Cedric claimed.

"Okay, so we are hunting a telepath or two enhanced by magic for the express purpose of weaponizing repressed human negativity. That doesn't get us any closer to stopping the deaths," said Sage.

"It's one of the missing pieces. Weapons need to be tested. In this case, it needs to be done without anyone seeing a pattern. All the targeted homeowners didn't have working doorbell cameras, including me. So, the tester uses ordinary people— old, young, men, women—in isolated clusters so the contagion can't spread in the population," I said.

"I thought the idea was for it to spread," queried Sage.

"Not here. Somewhere else, say North Korea, Russia, or China. The telepath probably tailored his mental commands to ensure the effects were contained. He also must have varied them to create a combo platter of murderers, victims, and suicides," I explained.

"So now what?"

"We start looking for a Mr. Garibaldi: a bald, dumpy middle-aged man who may haunt a house somewhere in my neighborhood," I replied. "We should also check our data bases for Doctor Zappfe, Mr. Mainlander, and a Mr. David Benatar."

"And if we find this Garibaldi, what then? One look from him, and we'll be at each other's throats."

"I am betting that polarized sunglasses like the

kind old people wear will afford some protection. We'll carry pocket mirrors should that fail. We will play Perseus to his Medusa," I offered.

Sage said, "The Medusa allusion seems apropos. But instead of turning men and women in their entirety to stone, our gorgon simply petrifies their hearts, and they do the rest."

***

When my captain discovered I had not taken bereavement leave, he sent me home.

"I can understand how you feel, but in this time of mourning you need to be with your family. Think of your wife's mother and father, her sisters, her cousins, nieces, and nephews. When you have dealt with that, I will consider letting you back on the case. But until you get right with them and yourself, I'm not letting you near the investigation."

I took his words with a grain of salt. I went to the viewing at the funeral home and did my duty as the grieving husband and father. Handshakes, hugs, and "sorry for your loss" with one eye on the bereaved and the other on my case.

On the second day of the viewing, I got a call from Sage.

"Bring your shades and get your ass down here. There's a riot in Times Square. Looks like the work of Mr. Garibaldi." I made my excuses and casually left the funeral home, then sprinted to my car and drove like a madman. I took the Battery Park Tunnel which runs under the East River and connects Red Hook in Brooklyn to Battery Park in Lower Manhattan. I tried driving up Eighth Avenue. Traffic was bumper to bumper. Presumably, the melee in Times Square was affecting the flow. I ditched my car and jogged to Times Square.

There were bodies everywhere. Over a thousand people had taken the plunge from The New York Times Tower, the Biltmore, the Hyatt, the Weston, and virtually every other skyscraper surrounding the plaza. Here and there, a dismembered or bludgeoned body peppered the fallen, adding the color of less dramatic suicides to the grim tableau.

I stepped over body after body to reach Sage who was talking to a man sipping a latte outside the Starbucks. He wore a high-end three-piece suit. But as to his face, it seemed at times blurred and indistinct. As if he were projecting his essence in from another location.

"Is this your partner? The both of you must try this full-bodied dark roast coffee. Bold and robust, the epitome of artistry in its blend of balanced and lingering flavors."

"Sir, please tell my partner what you saw," Sage said.

"Neither of you were born when the Stock Market crashed in 1929 on what became known as Black Thursday. On that day, distraught bankers and investors were leaping out of high-rise windows and plummeting as quickly as the stock market itself. It was truly something to see. Much the same happened here a few hours ago but on a much larger scale. First, the chairs and desks crashed through the windows creating openings for the jumpers. Then they leaped into space. But they didn't fly like leaves on the wind but fell with the gravity of balloons filled with strawberry yogurt. The impact sent chunks and gore in all directions. They came in wave after wave.

"The airborne suicides were complemented by the mass murders at street level. The cops poured out of the Times Square Police Annex and shot everything in sight. People attacked one another like wild animals. The costumed characters that normally pose with tourists for photographs got into the act killing of another. Micky kicked Minnie to death. Elmo strangled Spiderman. Buzz Lightyear stabbed Darth Vader to death with a fork. I saw a blind man bite a police horse, a hooker eat her own foot, and a man drink blood from a decapitated head."

"I'm surprised you didn't join the party and go crazy like everyone else," I said.

"I'm in this world, but not of it. So, fads and mass hysterias tend not to affect me. Besides, I have learned various methods of spiritual detachment over the years. They insulate me from the madness of the crowd, irrespective of the insanity's potency. When the time comes for me to see the pale horse and feel the flowers growing over me, I will be ready. Like the cover of an old book, its contents torn, and lettering stripped, I shall lie, food for worms. Will the work be lost, or will it appear once more in a more elegant edition? Who can say?" he soulfully exclaimed.

"So, you don't know how this came to be?"

"Why, I would know this handiwork anywhere. It's the Evil Eye. I suspect this outbreak is one in a series of tests to determine its efficacy in large population centers. So much more insidious than a mere virus or chemical weapon. After all, how do you fight something that has no discernible physical signature?"

I tried to put him in cuffs. But every time I reached for his hands, my hands passed right through them.

"I can't let you do that. Besides this unraveling has acquired a momentum all its own. Taking me into custody would change nothing."

Then he simply vanished.

Sage sighed, "I have a bad feeling that this thing is a lot bigger than we thought. I suggest you go back to the nuthouse and talk to our friendly neighborhood psychopath while I do a digital trace on Mainlander and Garibaldi."

***

Back at the Mid-Town psych ward, I found the Kraken waiting for me with a shit eating grin on his face.

"What's the good word, Dick Tracy?"

"I need you to look into your crystal ball and find something that will help me track down either Garibaldi or Mainlander."

"Sure. But I don't think you'll like what I must show you."

The walls of the cell began to flutter then undulate. A moment later, I was looking in on the same research facility I had seen before. Zappfe and the mystic Mainlander were seated at a table having drinks.

"I must say Phillip, the test results were even better than I had expected. The Times Square Massacre proved to be the cherry on the sundae. I believe we are ready to deploy our Momento Mori telepaths to Russia and China. The algorithms indicate complete extinction of the populations of both countries within a month. We could not have done it without your help."

"Thank you. I do try to accommodate customers like your superior Mr. Benatar."

"Like? Whom else have you helped?"

"Why your adversaries, of course: Russia and China."

"I don't follow."

"Did you honestly believe that we would hand over the ultimate weapon of war and expect nothing in return? A weapon that can extinguish the people of an entire nation without the need for boots on the ground or planes in the air. One that does no harm to the nation's infrastructure or eco-system. Surely you cannot be that naïve."

"I assumed you and your plans had been vetted by Mr. Benatar."

"They most certainly were. You see, he is a rather morbid fellow with a shuddering hatred of human life. He believes that human existence is a nightmare such that the ideal population size is zero.

So, when we approached him with our plan to eradicate the human race, he was only too eager to join and fund the conspiracy."

"How did he get so twisted?"

"He spent his entire life bluffing himself that the acquisition of money and power were desirable ends in themselves, and once in hand, they would give him happiness. Somehow, he saw through all the ballyhoo of positive thinking and realized that man is nothing more than a blemish on the earth. Or so the story goes. My feeling is that he is the corporate version of the political dictator addicted to power. Such a creature is always on the hunt for more, and no power is greater than the ability to exterminate one's own kind, to erase millions of years of evolution in one fell stroke. In any event, he threw in with us, and the rest is, as they say, history. Once your kind removes itself from the game board, we will take over."

"What about me? I found the telepaths and trained them. I did your dirty work and now you mean to throw me under the bus. Another body for your killing fields."

"Stop being a drama queen. You act like death is a bad thing. In your culture, birth is celebrated, and death is mourned. But you have it backwards. It makes more sense to mourn birth and celebrate death. If we went to the graveyard, knocked on the coffins, and asked who wants to rise again, the answer would be a thunderous 'Once was more than enough.' The dead know that while existence may have its moments of joy, it is mainly an exercise in pointless suffering. Your brief moment on earth is a very small thing compared with the nothingness before your birth and that after your death."

The images on the wall faded. Before I could say anything, I got a call from Sage.

"Dude, it's nuts here. I'm hiding under a desk in the precinct because everybody's gone crazy shooting up the place. I think the sunglasses are giving me immunity from the Evil Eye. But they're not making me bulletproof."

"Lay low for now. If you can, stay sheltered inside the building because things may be even worse on the street. I'm on my way."

He was stuck in a habitat of slaughter and all I could offer was a cradling illusion that renounced the inescapable truth he was as good as dead. And I was too. Either we would be killed or kill ourselves. There was no cure, no governor's reprieve at the last minute. For this soul sickness, this *morbus sacer* did not derive from the human world but from enigmatic spheres beyond the reach of science. Once infected by the glance of another, the demonic effects were inevitable. And where there had been a handful of controlled infections, the global outbreak was now under way. Where man had previously been a wolf to his fellow man in unpredictable ways, there was now a certainty that *Homo homini lupus* was now humanity's irrevocable trajectory.

As I left the facility, I donned my polarized sunglasses. I made sure my makeshift headband was secure so they would not slip off in a firefight or whatever other form of violence came my way.

231

***

Outside, Manhattan had become a killing field. As I drove, people leaped from skyscrapers and stabbed one another on the streets. Cars caromed into pedestrians, while pedestrians attacked moving cars with bottles and bricks. If someone got in my way, I ran them down. When they jumped on my car, I drew my Glock and shot them through the windshield or the roof. I hit cars. Other cars hit me. By the time I reached the Brooklyn Precinct my car looked as if it had survived the demolition derby at Raceway Park.

I always kept a loaded AR-15 in my trunk for emergencies. I never expected that I would be pointing it at fellow officers who were stark raving mad. But as soon as I drove up to Headquarters, I came under fire. I popped the trunk from the inside, slid out the driver side door and inched my way to my car's rear under a hail of bullets. I reached inside the trunk and grabbed the rifle along with some extra magazines. Assuming a prone position and watching the station from beneath my car, I saw several sets of legs moving toward my position. So, I shot them, hitting ankles and calves. Once the officers were down, I finished them with head shots.

I got up and raced toward the front door, zig zagging and firing as I went. There were bodies everywhere. The ones with head wounds were still holding the guns they had used to explode their heads. Others were riddled with bullet wounds from head to toe. I got on my phone and called Sage but got no answer.

I stepped over more bodies as I moved through the building. I could hear screams and shouts coming from the jail cells in the basement. I headed downstairs. As I did, I heard gunshots. When I opened the door, I found Sage. He was not wearing any eye protection. So, it was no surprise he had just executed all the prisoners.

He saw me and pulled the trigger. But his clip was empty. He threw his gun at me and charged. He moved too quick for me to fire a round. He slammed into me, and we both hit the ground. I expected punches or an attempt at strangulation. But instead, he tried to bite into me with his mighty equine teeth. I had my hands around his neck. Although I was resigned to choking him to death, and did my level best to do so, his mania was so puissant that his head kept coming closer and closer to mine. His snapping jaws caught my sunglasses and splintered them in two. They dangled to the side but were so large they still covered my eyes. I did the only thing I could do. I snapped his neck. When I did, he fell into me and knocked the glasses from my face. I was out of breath and full of regrets. So much so, I didn't see a wounded officer staggering my way. Our eyes met. And whatever baleful influence was in his glance communicated itself to me.

I shot him of course. But the damage had been done. My mind became a seething cauldron filled with a vile stew of self-loathing. I saw—really saw-

-the impossibility of ever adequately accounting for my happenstance existence, and the futility of all human effort given that we are ruled by implacable laws which nothing can repeal.

No longer hobbled by the pathological optimism of my kind, no longer blinded by its fabulous illusions, I saw my true self. A carcass rotting on the bone waiting to die. To confirm that diagnosis, I pulled out my Medusa mirror and saw the skull beneath my skin grinning back at me. I heard the music of a thousand graveyards vibrating in my blood. Soon, I would join the pasty specters loitering among the tombstones. I only need put my gun in my mouth and pull the trigger. Then and only then would the nightmare of my being finally be over. A minor but necessary contribution to the conspiracy against humanity.

## Amoeba

## B.F. Vega

Lysandra let go of the rope. She fell into the pond with a huge splash that reached all of us and drenched the grill I had just gotten started.

"Lys!" I called in annoyance.

She surfaced spitting water up into the air like she was a fountain topper.

"You put the fire out!" I yelled at the eighteen-year-old who was currently giggling like she was eight.

"You shouldn't have put it so close to the pond!" she yelled back before diving down into the murky water.

When she surfaced again I said, "Fine. I'm taking the grill back up by the parking lot. When you get tired of splashing around I'll be there."

"Whatever!" she yelled and splashed some water in my direction.

Her best friend Kayla was much better behaved than my daughter. She was sitting on a log, dipping her feet into the pond.

"Why can't you be more like Kayla?"

"Cause Kayla's boring!" she said with a grin and splashed her best friend. I left as a full water splashing war escalated.

It was warm for October. There was a mugginess to the air that usually preceded a storm but there were no clouds anywhere. The sky was so blue it sometimes seemed like it was made of glass. The girls finally joined me at the picnic table. They were both completely soaked.

"How are you going to get home?"

"In the truck with you," my sassy daughter replied.

"Not like that you aren't," I said indicating the drippiness of their beings.

"Mom. We'll be plenty dry by the time we finish all this food. Besides, Dad left his jacket in there, I'll just sit on that if I'm still drippy."

She and Kayla proceeded to eat their way through more food than was served at a typical southern funeral. Where they put it I had no idea.

Both girls were tall and lean. Kayla played water polo and Lysandra had been the captain of her senior volleyball team. They were both now at the local community college doing a semester without sports so that they could get their academics established, but I knew that both girls missed it.

When we got back to our house, Kayla stole some of her own clothes back from Lys for her drive home. Michael was working the third shift that night so it was just Lys and I for dinner.

I suggested we order out but she said that she wasn't feeling super hungry and had tired herself out eating all the food I had made earlier.

I laughed and tried not to worry about her sudden

lack of appetite. She looked a little pale, but since she said that she was tired I put it down to that.

"Okay sweetie. Well, get some rest, okay?"

"Yeah. Night Mom," she said and padded down the hallway to the bedroom she had occupied since she was three days old.

I stayed up a while watching reruns of *Murder, She Wrote* until my eyelids were too heavy. On my way to bed I stopped by Lysandra's room. She was snoring slightly, with the covers almost completely covering her head. I smiled and pulled the door closed behind me.

The next morning I got up to make breakfast, being careful not to wake Michael who had gotten in at almost three that morning. Lysandra's door was still closed but I figured that she had gotten up to go for a run as usual.

I decided to make waffles for some reason. They were her favorite and I guessed that she would be starving after skipping dinner the night before.

As the batter was resting and bubbling for maximum fluffiness I heard Lysandra's door open.

I glanced at the clock on the microwave and saw that it was almost nine. Lysandra had always been an early riser. Nine was like noon for her.

"Lys, honey?" I called out, worried.

I heard a few footsteps and then I heard someone fall against the wall.

"Lys?!" I stuck my head around the kitchen door to look down the hall. Lysandra was trying to stand back on her feet. She was using the wall for leverage. As I watched, she fell again.

"Lys!" I screeched, running to her. "Michael help!" I yelled to my sleeping husband.

Lys opened her eyes and looked at me.

"Mommy?" she whispered.

She hadn't called me mommy since she turned ten and Kayla had made fun of her for it. "Mommy, I'm…" her eyes unfocused as the first seizure hit her.

"Michael!" I screamed at the top of my lungs.

"What?" my husband finally said, running into the hallway.

"Call 911!" I yelled as I tried to hold my baby girl's head still.

The ambulance got there in under five minutes. They were able to stabilize her enough to get the tremors to stop. They were yelling questions at me. What had she eaten? Did she do drugs? Was there a history of seizures?

'No, no, no. Just help my little girl!" I begged.

"We're trying, ma'am."

One of the paramedics strapped Lysandra onto the board for transport. I saw him lean over and look at her ear. He blinked twice and looked up at his partner. I saw some sort of unspoken communication pass between them that caused a ring of ice to squeeze my heart.

"Ma'am, has she been swimming lately?" the paramedic asked.

"Yesterday at the old mill pond. Why?"

Instead of answering, the first paramedic turned to the second and said, "Call County. Tell them we might have a case. They could need the chopper."

"I'm coming with you," I said.

"No ma'am. Meet us at county medical. They will inform you of where to go next." And then they loaded my daughter up and raced off into the morning.

I don't know how Michael made my old truck do the fifteen-minute trip to the county hospital in ten minutes. I didn't care. If we had a jet it wouldn't have been fast enough for me.

We walked in and immediately were ushered into a barren room with three white chairs, white walls, and white linoleum. There was a tv high up on the wall playing a re-run of *Jeopardy*.

"I need you to wait here," the orderly who met us at the door said.

"Our daughter?" Michael asked.

"The doctor is on his way to speak to you," she said, adding, "Can I get you something? Coffee? Tea?"

"Coffee would be great. Thank you," Michael answered. I just shook my head. There was a feeling in my stomach like quicksand. I kept imagining that my insides were going to be sucked down through the gnawing emptiness I was beginning to feel. I knew that whatever was coming was going to be very bad.

After what seemed like an eternity, the orderly returned with coffee for Michael and handed me some water that I had asked for me. We thanked her and as she left a doctor entered.

"Mr. and Mrs. Weber?"

"Yes. How's Lysandra?" I asked, jumping up out

of my seat.

The doctor touched my shoulder gently and said, "Why don't you sit down? We have a lot to discuss. But I will tell you that right now she is alive and we are doing everything we can to keep her that way."

"Why wouldn't she be alive? She is a healthy eighteen-year-old. What is going on?" I cried out. Michael stood and grabbed me in a bear hug, before gently lowering me back into a chair.

The doctor waited until the worst of my crying had passed and I was wiping my eyes on the soft flannel of Michael's jacket.

"Lysandra is being airlifted to Atlanta in under ten minutes."

"Atlanta?" my husband asked.

"It's the top of the line for brain surgery, I promise you. If anyone can save her, it's them."

"Brain surgery?" I yelled, popping up onto my feet again.

"There's more," the doctor said, not quite meeting my gaze.

Both Michael and I stared at him. How could there be more than that?

"Even if they are able to save her. There is a large chance that she will not have the same cognitive brain function that she did."

"What? Why? What is going on?" Michael said.

"Mr. and Mrs. Weber, your daughter has been infected by a tiny parasitic larva. These infest the cranium of humans and can quickly eat through brain matter. Luckily for Lysandra, the paramedics who responded this morning had just completed training on new pathogens and vectors to be on the lookout for. They saw what looked like a tiny worm disappear down her ear canal and called ahead to alert us. If we can get the larva out fast enough she might live. But we don't know what is already lost."

I sat down hard on the plastic chairs as the impact of what the doctor was saying hit me. I heard a knock on the door but didn't look up. There was a soft murmur of voices. I couldn't make out what they were saying at first.

"Mrs. Weber?"

I looked up. A man wearing a dark suit under a physician's coat had entered the room.

"Yes?"

"I'm Dr. Sampson. I work for the CDC. I need to ask you some questions."

I looked up at Michael who nodded to me.

"What? What do you need to know?"

"Has your daughter been near a pond or lake or river lately?"

I nodded, remembering that the paramedic had asked me something similar. "Yeah, um. We were at the old mill pond yesterday."

"We? Did you swim as well?"

"No. I was cooking while Lysandra and Kayla were splashing each other. Why?"

"Who's Kayla?"

"Kayla Tregar. She's Lysandra's best friend," Michael answered him.

"And she was also in the water?" Dr. Sampson asked.

"Yes."

"And, just to verify, the old mill pond would be the pond that sits just east of the Vector Control offices?"

I nodded in the affirmative. My thoughts were foggy. I saw a few loose white threads on the back of Michael's jacket and raised my hand to brush them off. There were a lot of them. It seemed weird that he would have so many random strings on him.

"Mrs. Weber, what are you doing?" Dr. Sampson asked.

"There are all these strings on Michael," I answered as I started brushing them off. They just seemed to keep multiplying all over his back.

Dr. Sampson grabbed my hand. "Mr. Weber, have you been swimming?"

"No," Michael answered.

Dr. Sampson plucked one of the strings from Michael's back and looked at it very closely. I watched in horror as the string moved of its own accord and my brain suddenly realized what was all over my husband.

"Mr. Weber. I need you to calmly take off all your outer clothing. Doctor, Mr. Weber will need to be taken to a decontamination chamber and then we will need to do an MRI and check for parasites. Mr. Weber, do you happen to know how you came to be in contact with the larva?"

"No. I wasn't even around Lys until this morning when we called the paramedics and I wasn't wearing my jacket. It was in my wife's truck, in fact." He stopped and looked at me.

"Lysandra and Kayla were sitting on it yesterday

on the way home. The larva must have come from them."

"Okay," Dr. Sampson said calmly before stepping out of the room and yelling something to the nurse outside.

A million things happened at once. The room was flooded by orderlies and nurses. They pulled Michael's jacket and t-shirt, shoes, socks, and jeans off him, putting them in large plastic bags marked with a big bio-hazard symbol. They then rushed him out of the room and I was ushered in the opposite direction toward the emergency room. First I was escorted to a shower room where a nurse was waiting to check my hair and clothes and skin. I was instructed to shower quickly and then I was given some scrubs as my clothes were also taken away.

"Clean," I heard the nurse say when Dr. Sampson entered.

"Where can we find Kayla Tregar?" he asked me.

But I didn't have to tell them. We all heard the anguished yowl from the nearby emergency room entrance. Dr. Sampson and the nurse rushed out. I was right behind them. I turned a corner and could see the doctor holding open the big double doors that looked into the ER waiting room. Perfectly framed right inside the entrance of the hospital I could see Kayla's father sobbing and yelling with his daughter draped over his arms, her eyes open and bleeding onto the floor. I took a step forward but Dr. Sampson turned and saw me.

"No. Nurse. Get her into an isolation room right

now."

"Doctor?" I asked softly, not registering the fear in his voice. "Why is her blood… wriggling?"

Dr. Sampson turned and saw what I saw. As the blood ran down Kayla's face and hit the floor, small thread-sized pieces wriggled out of it in every direction.

"Full lockdown!" Dr. Sampson called and one of the ER nurses pushed a button that sounded an alarm.

The first nurse in a hazmat suit rushed past me. He had almost reached Kayla and her father when Mr. Tregar's eyes started to bleed and his knees seem to give out. He folded in half, dropping himself and Kayla into the puddle of wriggling blood and splashing it all over every surface and every person within five feet of him. Dr. Sampson had turned toward the ER and his body shielded me from the splash that hit him full in the face. I took a step backward and almost slipped in some of the blood that now dotted the linoleum. A hand grabbed me. I screamed, but it was just a nurse in a hazmat who had come to escort me to a cleanroom. This time I was shoved in the shower still in the scrubs I had been wearing. I hadn't felt any blood hit me, but I looked down at my feet in the blue paper booties and saw a single, now white thread slip off of them down the drain. I tore off every stitch of clothing and scrubbed my hair so hard that I ended up almost clogging the drain with all the hair I pulled out. However, that one larva was the only one I found.

When I got out of the shower the same nurse was waiting for me with new scrubs.

"I want to see my husband," I said.

"I'm not supposed to…" I could hear the screams from outside the door.

"Take me to my husband and then you can go help others."

There was a moment when the nurse looked indecisive but the door opened and a woman in scrubs stood there.

"Janice, I need help…" the woman said as the blood started running down her nose and out of her mouth.

"Brenda!" Nurse Janice yelled. "Hang on, okay?" She turned to me. "This way."

We both quickly stepped around the pool of blood forming on the floor. She led me down the hall to a room marked "private" and opened it with her key card. "Stay here," she ordered.

I saw that I was in some sort of observation room that looked into a quarantine room where Michael lay on a bed with no fewer than two doctors and six nurses working on him.

"Thank you," I turned to say but the nurse was gone and the door was closed.

I tried the handle and found that she had locked it. I turned back to Michael's room and saw the first nurse collapse. Then the second. More people in hazmat suits rushed into the room to try to evacuate the medical personnel. I saw the seizure hit Michael that had hit Lysandra that morning. But no one was watching him anymore as the doctors and nurses and the hazmat people started slipping in the wriggling blood that was slowly spreading and splashing on every surface.

I pounded on the plexiglass screaming.

One of the hazmat people saw me and I yelled Michael's name as loud as I could, pointing to the bed where my husband had stopped seizing and blood was pooling onto his pillows.

The hazmat person ignored Michael as the machine at his side started sounding a loud piercing tone. They got up to the window and closed the curtains, leaving me no way to see in and with only the company of the flatlining heart monitor.

I screamed and pounded, but eventually, my arms and lungs refused to put in any more work and I slumped down to the ground. Then I did something I hadn't done in years. I prayed. I don't know how long I was on that cold tile listening to the alarm in Michael's room as it was joined by first one then four then an uncountable number of other alarms signaling that every patient in the hospital was in cardiac arrest. It seemed like forever, begging whatever was out there to spare my little girl. Eventually, I heard some of the heart monitors turn off. It took a few minutes for complete silence to fall. There was now no sound at all. I strained my ears to listen and heard the slightest whisper of Kevlar on the tile then the door lock beeped.

I looked up as the door opened but did not recognize the man in the hazmat suit.

"Mrs. Weber?" he asked

"Yes. Where's Lysandra?"

"I will answer your questions, but I need you to come with me first. Here, you'll need this," he said, handing me a hazmat suit.

"Michael...." I said, gesturing toward the still blocked window.

"I know," he answered, "and I'm sorry, but for right now the priority is to get you out of here so that I can take you to your daughter, okay?"

"Is she alive then? Is she okay?"

"She's in surgery still. If you want to be there when she gets out I need you to get into that suit and follow me."

"Okay," I said, starting to try to get into the bulky outfit. I couldn't seem to make my legs work and my hands were shaking.

"Let me help," the man said and quickly helped me into the suit, taking almost my full weight as my poor legs were numb from sitting on my knees for so long.

"Thank you."

"You're welcome," he answered automatically. "Now I need you to follow right behind me. Don't look around, don't venture off, no matter what you see. It's for your own good, okay? We are headed to the elevators at the other end of the hospital that will take us up to the roof. In case something goes wrong, you should know that when we get out onto the roof we are going to be met by a decontamination squad. You will need to strip down again, then they will give you new scrubs before we get on the helicopter. Do you understand?"

"Then I get to see Lysandra?"

"Yes."

"That's all that matters."

"This way," he said and turned out to the hallway.

I followed close behind. I saw white and blue lumps everywhere. It took me a moment to realize that they were people in scrubs and lab coats curled up in the fetal position, dead on the floor. There was blood everywhere. A lot of it had started to dry and I wondered again how long I had been in the room.

"Dried blood isn't a concern," the man said as if he could read my thoughts. "The larva are aquatic, they can't survive if they dry out."

I wanted to ask how he knew. It occurred to me then that there seemed to be a lot of people who knew about, and in fact seemed to have been looking for, this parasite. I would have asked the man about it, but I then spotted a pool of still wriggling blood and concentrated on getting around it without touching anything.

We carefully walked down a hallway toward the elevators. I was so focused on trying not to touch any of the almost three dozen bodies that we encountered, while staying away from any still damp blood, that I didn't notice Dr. Sampson until the door of the elevator dinged and made an odd squishy sound when it opened.

The doctor sat in the hallway with his back against the elevator door, and the squishing was his hand being ground into the side cavity as the doors retracted. The blood from his nose and eyes had pooled in his open mouth where it had managed to stay liquid. When the elevator door moved him he slumped over and the blood leaked down onto the floor but it didn't wriggle with parasites like the rest of the blood I had seen.

His head had turned up at me and I could see that his eyes were already clouded from death. I don't know why but this man that I had only really known for a few minutes was the last straw. I was struck with the grim horror and sorrow and outrage and grief of the whole situation. Without thinking, I dropped to my knees.

"We need to go," the man beside me said, trying to pull me up and into the elevator car.

I pulled my arm out of his grasp and reached out to the man in front of me.

"Dr. Sampson…" I whispered as I tried to close his now white eyes. The gloves made it hard to do anything. Impulsively I pulled one off to try again.

"No!" my companion yelled.

But I had already reached out. When my hand touched his forehead I felt that it was already cool. My fingertips moved to his eyelids. I got a little closer to make sure I didn't poke him in the eye. Then his eyeball moved. The film on his lens separated and squiggled into the dozens of tiny worms that had obscured his dead irises. I felt the touch of them moving under my fingers as I closed his eyelids over them and watched them start to burrow out through the thin flesh.

I don't remember moving or screaming, but the next thing I knew I was sitting with my back against the cold metal of the inside of the elevator car and the door was closing in front of me.

As it closed I noticed that a small white string had fallen onto my hand and was starting to work its way under the elastic of the wrist of the suit, up toward my head. I screamed again. My companion reached down and pulled the suit arm up. Six little white strings were wiggling up my arm.

"Stay still!" he said as he produced a specimen cup from a bag he wore. He also had something like a tiny baster or a pipette with a larger than normal bulb that he used to carefully suction up the strings and deposit them into the specimen cup. He then produced a pen and wrote Culex Q. Larvae Patient A.

He then held it up to the light as I furiously started checking every inch of myself, sure that I could feel crawling on every atom of skin.

When we got to the roof the man handed the cup to another person in a full hazmat suit who put it in a biohazard marked container and got into one of two helicopters that were sitting on the roof.

I gladly went through the decontamination process. I was stripped and inspected for parasites then showered again. I scrubbed my skin red with my nails making sure there was no way that I missed any of the tiny worms. I was then given a fresh suit of scrubs that I inspected carefully before putting them on. When I was as satisfied as the technicians were that I was parasite free, I allowed them to escort me to a helicopter.

I could hear sirens below me, but I couldn't see anything. Finally, my companion joined me in the helicopter.

"Strap in," he said.

As I did, he gave the pilot permission to take off.

"What about all the others?" I asked, looking out at the dozens of people in hazmat suits still on the roof.

"They have work to do. They will collect more samples and then transport them to our lab in Atlanta where they will try and figure out… a lot of things," he explained, obviously breaking off from what he had meant to say.

The helicopter started its engine then and the sound of the blades obscured all other noise. My companion indicated a headset. I did a triple check of it before putting it on my ears. As I got it situated I was able to look down and out of the window beside me.

The sirens I had heard came from ambulances and police cars sitting in the hospital parking lot. Their drivers were laying on the ground in small groups. None of them were moving. As we rose, I could see that for a block around the hospital nothing moved. There were bodies here and there and then abruptly a large perimeter. Beyond the perimeter, I could see the National Guard and more hazmat people dealing with what looked like the rest of the town trying to get through the barrier at every side street.

As I watched, a person in the middle of the crowd that was closest to the hospital suddenly fell to the ground with no warning.

"Hell!" the man across from me said. "HQ, this is Agent Green. It looks like it's in the crowd."

I heard a response on my headset. A male voice replied, "Affirmative. Sending backup now."

As we flew away I saw large trucks and government vehicles racing to encircle the crowd containing the prone figure.

"What's going to happen to them?" I asked as we flew out of sight.

"They will isolate all of them, check for parasites, and deal with what they find. Hopefully, we can contain this to just your town," Agent Green answered.

"By containing, you mean that you are going to lock them in that town, don't you?"

"We have to get this contained. You saw how quickly it can kill."

"Over a thousand people live in my town. You're going to sentence them to death, aren't you?"

"If we can clear someone we will. They will be taken to a sterile environment for twenty-four hours and then released, but not home."

"And where are we going?"

"Atlanta. The main hospital for the Center for Disease Control. That's where Lysandra is."

He started to say more but the voice in our headset piped in asking for further information about containment and by the time he had finished giving orders we were landing and all I cared about was getting to Lysandra.

"The nurse will take you from here," Agent Green said as we landed. "I will stop in later and I promise to answer your questions."

Then he was gone. A woman in scrubs was guiding me toward the roof access to an elevator that would take me to my little girl.

"She's out of surgery," the nurse was saying as we walked. "The doctor will want to speak with you."

We walked through a door guarded by two men in uniforms with rifles and then down a long hallway that had sealed doors along its route. At the end, a doctor was waiting for us.

"Mrs. Weber?" he said

"Yes, how is she?"

"We were able to successfully remove the larval ball but unfortunately the larva had been feeding on her spinal column."

"What does that mean?"

"Well, we think that she has lost all mobility from her neck down."

"She's paralyzed?"

"We can't be sure yet, but it looks that way. Now, she's in a medically induced coma but it will do her good to hear your voice. Are you up to seeing her?"

"I would go through anything to hold my baby." I stared at him completely disgusted that he would even consider not allowing me in.

"Very well," he conceded and the nurse let me into the room where Lysandra was lying on a bed much like her father had not too long ago. But she was breathing and appeared to be sleeping peacefully. I didn't know how much I had been holding in until I touched her warm hand. I started sobbing.

I don't remember falling asleep, but I woke up as the sun was setting, still holding my daughter's hand. Agent Green was sitting in a chair across from me reading a magazine like this was a normal thing to do.

He looked up. "I promised to answer your questions. And you have more than earned the truth."

"Tell me what this is," I said, glaring at him.

"Have you heard of Naegleria Fowleri?"

"No."

"It's an amoeba that can cause large parts of the brain to disintegrate."

"Disintegrate?"

"I believe when the press reported on the last known case they used the term brain-eating amoeba."

"The brain-eating amoeba?" I asked, remembering the headlines I had seen a few years ago.

"Yes."

"But these are larva?" I was silent for a moment then remembered something. "On the sample bottle of that larva you got off me, you wrote Culex. That's a mosquito, right?"

"Yes. We think it's the Cules Quinquefascuatus larva. We aren't a hundred percent sure how the mosquitos got infected, but the amoeba appears to be using the larva to get into brain matter. We think this has altered what the larva are looking for to feed on."

"Feed? But you said all those dead people back there... when the blood dried that there wasn't danger."

"No, but the larva that were able to form larval balls in the brains of those infected didn't leak out with the blood. They will continue feeding until they are large enough to complete the transformation into adult mosquitoes, then the cycle will start all over again. It's why they kill so quickly, we think."

"But Lysandra?"

"Yes, you seem to have some sort of resistance to them and she seems to have some of your unexplained immunity. As soon as she arrived and we realized that there was something different about her we knew that we had to find her parents. It's why it was important enough to put a recovery team together to come get you."

"But there were larva on me."

"Mrs. Weber, when you pulled your hand away from Dr. Sampson's face originally, it was covered in larva. By the time you got into that elevator all but those six had fallen off and were apparently dead on the floor. Those six are being sent to our lab right now to see why they resisted whatever it is that makes you lethal to them. We will need blood samples from you as soon as possible, by the way."

"If I help will you be able to stop this? Will more people..." I couldn't go on. The sobs came from nowhere. The last time I had cried like this, Michael had held me. He was already dying by then. The thought made me cry harder.

"If it helps at all," Agent Green said, "we think that we were able to catch it fast enough to contain it to your town. As long as none make it out of there and we can work on your immunity then we can make sure no one else will suffer."

I sniffled, controlling my emotions as best I could. "I'll help."

"Good. Is there anything that you need right now?" he asked.

"A shower," I said, then remembered that the larva was aquatic. "Actually, I may never shower again."

He gave me a wry smile. "I promise it will be okay."

A nurse entered. "Agent Green," she said in a tone that made me look up at her colorless face and huge eyes.

"Yes?" he asked.

"Turn on the tv," she whispered.

He flicked on the tv that was mounted in the corner of the room. The news was reporting on a helicopter crashing into the Mississippi River. The ariel footage showed a helicopter broken apart all over the water.

"Sweet God, no," Agent Green whispered as the first body, still in their hazmat suit, was pulled from the water, covered in a white wiggling mass.

## The Fey

### Jason A. Wyckoff

The city was hushed and rust-sheened: the snow cast light orange; the twisted lattice of naked branches like brittle ash against the cinder sky; the hovering air harmoniously stained in smoldering hues incongruous with the chill. Cars and rooftops wore frozen veils, a courtesy to huddled mourners of the orange-entombed world well-hid behind blinds and curtains.

I'd once tried to describe such a night to my former father-in-law. He was born, raised, and died in rural Tennessee. To him, a well-lit night meant a clear sky and a full moon high above the horizon, casting fragile shadows in ghostly script across the blue earth. In the country, light from above was key.

In the city, it was the opposite. A low dome of cloud cover was required to reflect the pollution emanating from underneath, streetlights and porch lights and every excess left to burn unheeded. And if there was snow on the ground, the reflected glow would bounce up again, and back down again, back and forth, creating a translucent fog of color.

In either situation, the braggadocios claim would be that the light was so strong you could read a

257

newspaper by it. But who would go out into a magical night to catch up on current events, only to prove a point?

I did not go out. I was inside, peeking through a teardrop gap between the curtains, feeling the press of cold through the glass while I gazed at the placid uniformity of my smothered neighborhood. I'm not sure how long I'd been staring out the window before she appeared.

Running between streets, alongside my house and the one behind, was a one-way alley. Between that and its far mate (running the other way) was a tiny 'park', one lot wide. The park was an island studded with narrow birch and maple growing without plan. There was an accidental clearing fortuitously near the center into which a single bench had long ago been set and possibly never since occupied.

Even behind the shut window, I heard her before I saw her. As with the rebounding light, sound finds no rest on new-fallen snow; in fact, the dwarfing stillness can be an ally. Tinkling joy heralded her arrival. Then I saw her, moving between the trees on the island, lazily chasing her melodious laughter. A few seconds' observation crushed the hope that her weaving motion was drunken stumbling; she glided in diagonals effortlessly through eight inches of snow, twirling unerringly at each pivot, touching the trees with her fingertips only as she pleased, never to correct for distance or for support. And so I knew her laughter wasn't born from inebriation. Which meant, of course, that she would soon be dead.

A small, dark shape fell behind her: her hat. She spun with her arms stretched back and her coat cartwheeled free. I saw her face as she drew near the bench. She was young, but then they were all young, or appeared newly young as they approached death, skin tightening as their fixed smiles of pure delight shone beatifically. I suppose she was pretty.

Tufts of snow erupted as she kicked her boots free. She squatted behind the bench. She straightened and walked around it, and I could see her grooming habits. Her legs began to shake; her steps shortened. She crossed her arms behind her head and bent to remove her pullover. She dropped it unceremoniously. She laughed at the discarded garment.

She looked at the virgin snow in front of her as though noticing it for the first time. Her eyes widened and her mouth fell open with ecstasy. She knelt, and then stretched forward into a slow dive. She remained flat and straight for two minutes or more, and then she turned on her side, facing away, and drew her knees up, curling into a fetal position. She shivered for a while, or convulsed with rolling fits of laughter, I couldn't say which—but not for long. Thereafter she shook with small spasms between lengthening intervals of stillness. I don't know how long it takes for hypothermia to kill. She was skinny; does that matter? I was beginning to grow tired, and I was afraid I'd be up all night if I continued to watch her. I thought about putting on my boots and going out to check on her, though I lamented further disturbing the near-pristine snow. I admit, even at that late date, I thought it might be possible to help her.

*****

Cat. Boy. Eat. Ask. Run. Die. God. Fundamental things and basic actions are named early, their importance acknowledged through brevity, their original meanings distinct and singular. Even God. Just ask a believer.

Fey. An important word—fundamental—yet imprecise. By the word's length men assigned its weight (perhaps with uncomprehending prescience) yet struggled to elevate its primary meaning. A collection of three letters, with three definitions only marginally related until the terrible, perfect integration of the three careened into daily life. Small wonder it was adopted so quickly when the crisis began. First: doomed to die—by suicide. But also: in a strangely ecstatic mood—the primary symptom. Or possibly: otherworldly (in the sense of not of *our* world, though perhaps of *the* world, of old magic)—seen in the physical change brought on by an infection debated to be either a 'natural' contagion or an assault perpetrated by some 'others' who might be blamed for its spread (resulting in a confusing conflation of the adjective 'fey' with the noun 'fay' (meaning a fairy)). Soon, 'Fey' was blanketly applied to the condition, the description, the incursive aliens, and the human victims.

There must have been a clue in that amalgamation, something once understood, now forgotten—some vital connection as to why the word *fit* so well with our current apocalypse.

"You're late," Jennings said with mock sternness; likely the only real edge came from his consternation at himself for being foolish enough to show up on time. People still got emotional—very emotional at times, buckling under the strain—but few pretended anything 'normal' really mattered anymore. Still: habits endured. Jennings still styled his hair with gel, unfailingly and impeccably. He was resting an elbow on Tom Wolk's cubicle wall, the one next to mine, a mug of coffee in his hand. Tom, more rumpled, reclined on the black plastic hive-weave of his chair, facing away from his monitor. "Morning," he greeted.

I shook my coat off and hung it on the hook clamped to the cubicle wall.

"I was on the subway platform, waiting for my train," I began, explaining my tardiness.

Both men groaned before I could continue. "I can see where this is going," Jennings said.

"'Fraid so," I said. "I heard a commotion down by the tunnel at the 'rear' of the platform. Then the crowd parted a bit, and I could see two of them, waltzing together and laughing. Right away, a bunch of people abandoned the station and made for the escalators. I considered it myself for a second— marching five blocks over to catch the orange line—but I figured the time wasted would be about the same either way, and the slush on the sidewalk had just about soaked through my shoes as it was. I hate wet socks."

"Christ—you stayed, even knowing what was coming?" Tom asked.

"Shut your eyes and cover your ears, that's what I say," said Jennings. "What else could he do—try to stop them?"

"There's still no evidence it's contagious," Tom said.

"Doesn't matter," Jennings countered. "You ever seen someone try to get between one and their death? That's a faster way to buy the farm than catching the sickness, guaranteed. I saw on the news the other day some dumbass drowned trying to save one who'd driven her car into the reservoir. They always seem to find a way, and they don't care who's *in* the way."

I chuckled. "There was a guy the size of a defensive lineman near them who was *pissed*. Cursed up a storm the likes of which I have never heard. But even he wasn't trying to get between them and the tracks."

"Hell, no," Jennings affirmed.

"You didn't *watch* though, right? You moved away?" Tom asked.

"The queue thinned out," I said.

He was incredulous. "You moved *forward?*"

"If I was going to have to wait for a while on a stalled train, I wanted to make sure I got a good seat," I said. "Look, it's bleak, sure, I know that. But they weren't my first train-jumpers. That's why I always wait at the 'front' end of the platform. You don't get any on you there."

Jennings laughed, one clipped bark before he caught himself. He cleared his throat and said, "You might not be able to use that excuse much longer. I heard starting next week they're not even going to clean them off until the end of the run."

Tom huffed in disbelief. "That can't be true. They have to. It's a safety issue."

Jennings shrugged and grimaced. "Wasted time."

"My Aunt Sylvia stabbed herself in the heart with a screwdriver."

I hadn't notice Janice approach. I half-turned to include her. The tiger's-eye frames of her glasses seemed to grow right out of her curls. "I'm sorry," she said, "I overheard what you said about it not being contagious. But my Aunt Syl would never do such a thing."

"I meant only that there's no proof yet it's contagious through person-to-person contact," Tom said conciliatorily. "We all know it can affect anyone."

We didn't talk about the Fey around Janice. In part because she was one of the leftovers who reacted emotionally, in part because of Holli Bryce. Janice's 'good heart' made her just the sort of middle-aged woman whose indulgent fandom drove her to obsess over ingenue pop stars for some reason.

Understandably, there was great confusion when the worldwide rash of suicides began. The hysteria was made worse by the fact that so many of the suicides occurred publicly. And yet, in the early going, many of the dead could not be identified. To some, it seemed almost conspiratorially mysterious that many of the 'acts' were so grievous as to leave bodies unrecoverable. These factors, combined with the strange, almost elfin appearance of the perpetrators (or victims, depending on the speaker) led to a proposal (quickly embraced by a surprisingly large portion of the populace) that those harming themselves were not human at all, but that they were a forgotten magical race vomited back into the public eye in this tragic manner because of accelerating climate collapse. To others, the conclusion seemed stupid and impossible, but, as such, in line with most current events.

One of the supporting claims of this hypothesis was an extrapolation from the problem of the victims' anonymity: the fact that no one of *note* had yet died in this manner. It was as though the public needed the sacrifice of a celebrity to make it real.

As all the suicides appeared vibrant and deliriously happy in their final moments, it was perhaps inevitable a youth movement fetishizing these alien dead would develop. Morbidity had new 'juice'. Into all this fell the previously scheduled release date of Holli Bryce's new album, a stab at respectability and seriousness for the star transitioning to maturity. The album tanked. Who knows what Holli actually believed about herself— if she felt actual kinship with the lovely and doomed because of what she was suffering publicly or if she was simply too shallow to recognize her own vanity and opportunism. What is certain is that she looked aged beyond her years and the harrowing fear in her eyes as she took cyanide at a press conference suggested she thought somebody would stop her. Or save her. Or do anything at all. Perhaps realizing her manager would allow it to happen was what pushed her to follow through with it.

She was lambasted by the media, tweet-flayed by the hip-to-death youth which she sought to impress. The abuse was as cynical as the intent Holli was accused of having.

Janice might have been her only remaining defender.

Of course, soon after, people who were known and loved throughout all social strati began to kill themselves, and some who had already died were identified long after the fact—as the morphological change brought on by the condition became more widely considered (and applied to numerous 'missing persons' cases). A new theory developed that this was an attack; that the 'original' (unidentifiable) Fey were not just suicide bombers but contaminating suicide *bombs*. They were to blame for 'turning' normal people, and responsible for the awful results which followed—though which of the Fey belonged among the accused 'they' was impossible to parse in gatherings of strangers.

The debate raged without flagging—was this an infection or an incursion? Was there a war on, perpetrated by earthly spirits whose weapon was an outwardly-spiraling compulsion towards suicide detonated by demonstrating like acts? Or was it 'just' tragic mass hysteria ravaging the world's populace, 'natural' madness which weaker minds, unable to assimilate the destruction it wrought, spruced up with fantastic trappings? Every conversation wound around to the questions—not only who was responsible for the deaths, but even who was doing the dying?

Likely an aversion to that recurring trap was what prompted Jennings to say, "Well, I'd better go see if there's anything I can get done today."

Janice frowned. "Sorry to break up the party."

"Oh, no, it's nothing like that," Jennings said unconvincingly. "Those purchase orders aren't going to request themselves."

No, they weren't, and they weren't going to be approved, either. Less and less was getting done each day. The efforts of those hardy souls still applying themselves ran headlong into the indifference of others. In that, I suppose only the scope was unusual.

After he left, Janice asked Tom and I, "Are either of you traveling for the holidays?"

It was a clunker of a question. Nobody wanted to put their lives in the hands of a pilot, and confidence in fellow drivers at high speeds was nearly as low.

"Portland is too far to drive," Tom said flatly.

I tried to smile encouragingly. "You?"

"No, but my son and his fiancé are coming up from Charlotte."

She seemed genuinely cheered at the thought. "Won't that be nice," I said.

"You're welcome to join us for Christmas dinner if you don't have other plans," she offered.

"That's very gracious of you," I replied, "but I won't be available."

***

"Sorry to break up the party," Jennings drawled in mockery of Janice.

Tom and I chuckled weakly in acknowledgement. Viv, Tom's wife, was puzzled by our amusement. "I don't get it."

"It's a work thing," Tom explained. "There's a woman there who's a bit of an Eeyore."

The Luffords were action-oriented optimists. I'm sure they thought keeping on with their annual holiday party was exactly the sort of thing everyone needed in such trying times. Jim Lufford was a former co-worker. I used to have a harmless crush on Jim's wife, Margot. Not so much anymore. Back when we worked together, the party was an even split between their 'work' and 'church' friends; now the scale dipped to the far side. We'd meet and re-introduce ourselves every year and try to remember if the other had kids or not, and then drift back to our natural groupings. There were fewer people this year, no surprise. I suppose those sending regrets could blame the weather. Our little group was on the dining room side of the counter partitioning the kitchen. We had our backs to a tall, shallow bay window. I kept alternating setting down my beer and my small plate of tiny meatballs and devilled eggs and such on the holly-print tablecloth. I hated trying to eat at parties; I don't know why I bothered with it.

"I see you made it *here* on time," Jennings sneered jocularly at me.

"That's because he came here with us," Tom said. "After three evasive answers when I asked if he was coming tonight, I knew I'd have to drag him out of his house."

"Late for work, were you?" Viv asked.

"There was a delay at the train station this morning."

Viv's face sank and she tilted her head. "Oh, no, not...?" she moaned.

"A two-for," I said.

Jennings nearly choked on his punch trying not to burst out laughing. Tom hid his eyes behind his hand. "But that's *terrible*," Viv said. "You shouldn't make light of it!"

"No, of course not," I said. "I don't mean it that way." I didn't know what else to say in my defense, so I said, "There was one outside my house last night." I began to raise a sweet gherkin to my mouth, but realized I'd have to explain, so I set it back on my plate and set the plate back down on the table to be abandoned.

"Jesus, Boone, you're turning into a magnet," Jennings chided me.

"What—what did he do?" Viv asked. She cradled her empty glass with two hands.

"She," I corrected. "Exposure. She stripped naked and laid down in the snow."

Tom weighed her fate with his eyebrows. "Not too bad, considering."

"Tom," Viv gasped.

He shrugged. "Well, really—for both parties involved. The things we've all seen." He shook his head.

"I thought about going out to see if I could do anything," I said.

"Like what?" Jennings asked. "Get one in while she was still warm?"

Viv grimaced. "Jesus," she whispered.

I said, "I thought maybe I could help her."

"But you know you couldn't have done anything." The new speaker was Margot, who had drifted within earshot.

Her hair was shorter than last I'd seen her, only down to her shoulders. I thought about complimenting her even though I didn't like it, but instead I kept to the subject. "It was the manner of her death which made me consider it. It's usually so violent and immediate. No second chances. I wondered if, maybe, she might reach a point very near death where the compulsion might run its course and… I don't know… release her."

"If she was human at all," Jennings pointed out. He sidled up beside Margot. His intentions were perhaps less harmless than mine once were.

"Oh, *that* again." Margot rolled her eyes. "I'm sorry, I don't see how anyone can believe that alien elf nonsense."

"Some say," Tom droned in a cartoonish New England country accent, "that it's the spirit of the earth itself doing a wee gallows-dance."

Fake accents had become employed frequently.

With an accent, one could say a truth without according any conviction to it. Or you could use an accent to announce you were going to say something funny, so listeners could be on guard not to laugh. One belief was that giddiness and frivolity themselves invited the infection or lowered your resistance or... something. Most theories on the Fey were inexact.

As if on cue, a burst of laughter rang from the living room, quickly crushed in the sudden, dread silence which followed.

"Sorry," someone murmured.

"No worries!" I heard Jim Lufford call from somewhere else, a bit too loud, over-compensating.

"What was your worst?" Margot asked the group, a topic guaranteed to quash any errant joviality. It would have seemed a grossly inappropriate choice of subject from anyone other than one of our hosts.

'Oh, God," Viv said, turning green. "Isn't there anything else to talk about?"

"There really isn't," Tom muttered consolingly. I could tell he was starting to think it was a mistake to come, or at least to bring Viv.

"All this 'fey' shit will run its course," Jennings said. "Just like everything else does. This time next year we'll be back to..." He paused, seemingly genuinely flabbergasted at not being able to recall a 'normal' topic of conversation. I think if he hadn't overextended himself, his first thought might have steered the conversation away. Instead, he let the air right back out of the balloon.

In the void, Margot challenged me, "You first. Since you're the 'magnet'."

It was an easy choice. "I think, like a lot of people, my worst was my first. Though it still holds up on more than just the shock of that first time. For a while, I had thought it was one of the *very* first, if only because I hadn't heard about any others before then."

"Self-important much?" Jennings jibed. "It's not enough to be a magnet, you have to be ground zero, too?"

I shook my head. "I just wasn't aware, that's all—but it *was* early on. So everyone who noticed the man sitting alone in the booth laughing to himself—this was at the Texas Roadhouse out by the Old Mill office park—well, me and everybody else I'm sure thought he was drunk or listening to something funny on an earbud. Or maybe off his meds, though he didn't look shabby. Still, he was 'off' enough that his server just about ran away after she dropped his meal in front of him. I kept an eye on him. He stared at his steak, eyes wide, big smile—you know the drill—had to be for five minutes solid, not doing anything but laughing now and then. I spied the server and could tell she was weighing the merits of asking him if everything was okay."

I mimed the next part as I told it. "Then, suddenly, he grabbed the steak in two hands, lifted it up and took a big bite. He chewed maybe three or four times, and then laughed again, open-mouthed. And then he stuck the whole thing in. He didn't try to fold it over to cram into his cheeks or anything like that. He just forced the slab straight into his throat. His fingers pushed in up to his first knuckles.

"The server screamed. There was a commotion as someone tried to give him the Heimlich. My view got blocked after that, so I don't know what all happened. But he choked and died. One of the managers took my food from me and boxed it up. When I got home, I saw she'd thrown several coupons in the bag."

Viv was tearing up.

"I'm sorry," I said, "that story went on too long"—as though the length of my narrative was the offense.

"It's all too much," she sniffled.

Tom put his arm around Viv's shoulders. "We might have to go," he said. "Can you manage?"

"Yeah, sure. I'll get Jennings to drive me home." Only then did I notice Jennings had meandered away from our group. Likely the offense for him *had* been the duration of my monologue.

Then it was just me and Margot. We sat on the ledge of the bay window. A new cluster of meek revelers whom I didn't know huddled around the table. We were comfortably walled off.

"Have you ever seen a jumper?" she asked.

"Not up close. But I've heard about them."

She nodded. "They don't fall flat. You wouldn't think it would make a difference, but—bear in mind, I have no frame of reference outside of movies and TV—but the way they *crumple* on impact..." She shuddered. "And you can hear the big bones snap. It isn't just 'splat'." She threw back her drink. "I guess the real question is, what the hell are 'real' suicides doing looking down?"

"I'd read somewhere that every jumper who survives says the same thing: the instant they're in free fall, they regret their decision and wished they weren't about to die. Presumably, the 'successful' ones think the same thing. So, the Fey, 'standing' upright, going down feet first... I suppose they don't care, which is odd in its way. Because, really, at that point, the ground is the only thing you have left to look forward to, right?"

She shrugged. "Or everything else. The ground is inevitable. Please tell me you're not trying to guess what the Fey are thinking."

"You haven't? Not even once? You haven't wondered what it feels like when that compulsion takes over, or what leads up to it?"

"Are you worried you're being left out?"

I looked her in the eye. I could see her fear. I think I even knew what it was—the fear that two people who knew each other could still never guess what the other was thinking, and that the divide only widened when things fell apart. She touched my leg.

Her voice cracked as she began, but she soon conquered it. "Here's what I know. The world is ending, and the party is in full swing. As best as can be expected, anyway. If you can be quick about it, we can get away to the bedroom and be back before anyone notices."

"I don't think I could manage that," I said.

273

She raised an eyebrow coyly. "Being quick?"

"The whole thing," I said, and her eyebrow drooped.

***

I didn't want to stay much longer after that and Jennings was just getting started, so I decided to walk home. It was only a bit more than a mile. I lamented having the wrong shoes on, but the night was warmer than last, and their street was clear, so I walked between the rows of cars lining the slow sloping avenue the Luffords lived on. It was one-way coming from behind me, but I reasoned I should be able to hear the susurrus of wet tires and see the glare of headlights spread before me long before any vehicle drew near, and there was such little traffic anyway.

A block up from Main Street I smelled the funk of natural gas as I passed a narrow alley which ran between two brown brick 'double' townhouses. I paused. There were lights on in both sides abutting the alley. I crept into the alley and identified the building to my right as being the source of the smell, though I couldn't tell if the leak came from outside or in. I stepped up over the low, cement block wall and climbed three clean-swept stairs onto the porch. It seemed that every light in the townhouse was on, blaring yellow on wan, cream-colored walls. The curtains were open.

There was a tall man seated on the side of the couch farther from the window, his head tipped back, with the back of the couch in the crook of his neck. The position exposed his neck and forced his mouth open, so I could not tell if his was an expression born of glee or of gravity.

With her feet towards the couch, her body perpendicular to it, a woman lay face down on an orange, coiled carpet. A young girl was on her back, almost as though she'd been piggy-back riding before they'd collapsed together. So I couldn't see any of them to be sure. Could a whole family be Fey? Or was this the work of one, with the decision acceded to by the other parent? There didn't appear to be an effort at constraining any party. Who posed this family snapshot?

"I wouldn't knock on that door," a voice called.

I turned and saw a portly older man on the porch of the townhouse on the other side of the alley. He was in a bathrobe and slippers, apparently having just emerged from the door behind him, though I hadn't heard.

"I wasn't going to," I said.

"One spark off that aluminum frame and the whole block will go up," he snarled. "You'd better leave it alone. I called the gas company. But who knows if they're even coming? I go to sleep tonight, I'll probably wake up dead in pieces two blocks over. Asshole Swedes!"

"They're Swedish?" I asked, unsure if I'd heard him correctly.

He harrumphed. "*Socialists*. All Swedes are socialists. They ever teach you that in *school*?"

I stared at him. A pop sounded in the distance,

followed by a sinking sound, and then all the lights went out up and down the street. I thought I heard a distant ironic cheer from the Luffords.

"Figures! Gas is working but they can't keep the electric on!" The man turned to go back inside. Before he closed the door, he glared back at me. "Well?"

I glanced back at the picture window, now black, and then I strode back to the street as the old man watched.

After turning onto Main Street, I was able to walk on the wide sidewalks without much difficulty. There was a bit of traffic, but nobody else was out by the shuttered boutiques and coffee shops at this time of night, in this weather, except for a skinny man with a weak chin, wearing a hoodie and smoking while he shuffled under a can light in front of a chocolatier (apparently the power outage was localized).

As I drew near, he turned his head without lifting his eyes and muttered, "Smoke? Smoke? What'ch'you want? I got it."

I made a dismissive motion with my hand. "Not my thing," I said.

He glanced up and down the street. There was a gap in the traffic running beside us. "There's something for everybody. And it's cheap now. Everything's dirt cheap, like you wouldn't believe."

I had passed him by this point, but I stopped. Not because I wanted anything from him, but I was curious about what he'd said. It would seem to me that supply lines for his sort of product should be drying up simultaneously with an exponential increase in demand.

"I would think it would be going the other way," I said.

"Naw, naw, man." He stepped closer, fidgeting. "Everybody's too afraid to feel good." He stepped closer again. "Shit, I'll straight up *give* you something to take the edge off if you promise to come back next week."

It wasn't the thought that he was the world's worst drug dealer that made me laugh louder than I had in a month, it was those words, 'next week'. It struck me later that maybe he was just using that line to get closer so he could jump at me with whatever he kept in his pocket. But maybe the offer was genuine — desperation makes life nonsensical. Either way, in normal circumstances, laughing in a dealer's face would be an open invitation to violent reprisal. But instead, my laugh slapped him backwards. His hood slipped back as he recoiled with fear. I laughed again unashamedly as he turned and scampered into an alcove.

Traffic thinned further as the lots widened beside me: fire station, church, bank. I turned onto my street, followed its curve out of sight of Main. They hadn't cleared my street, but I could walk in the ruts. Two blocks from my house, I froze stock still. Three dogs crossed the street half a block ahead: A pincer and a lab, with a small, white wirehair, old-lady dog struggling to keep up behind them, its belly dark with mud. There were many stray dogs now. I waited until I thought they were out of earshot and then continued on my way.

I stopped at the meager island park beside my house. I could see the lump of the woman who died there the night before. Had I forgotten to call the city? No one else seemed to have noticed. There were no other tracks in the park but hers.

I walked between the trees. I felt the snow seep into my shoes, and I became morose. I arced around in front of the dead woman, facing her, facing my house. Hip and shoulder were jutting, blue-veined stone. I looked up; the sky was clearing. Clouds fluttered free of their crisscrossed masts and drifted from view. Far, far beyond, our nearby neighbors in the infinite hailed us indifferently, lighthouses from too-distant shores. The special smell of water fallen from icicles kissed me. I squatted. I scooped the snow out from in front of her face. I grabbed a stray lock of hair and snapped it back. I bent lower and looked into her eyes. I searched her frost-burst, null and empty eyes and I did not see any magic in them.

Not one goddamned bit.

**Also from Red Cape Publishing**

**Anthologies:**

*Elements of Horror Book One: Earth*
*Elements of Horror Book Two: Air*
*Elements of Horror Book Three: Fire*
*Elements of Horror Book Four: Water*
*A is for Aliens: A-Z of Horror Book One*
*B is for Beasts: A-Z of Horror Book Two*
*C is for Cannibals: A-Z of Horror Book Three*
*D is for Demons: A-Z of Horror Book Four*
*E is for Exorcism: A-Z of Horror Book Five*
*F is for Fear: A-Z of Horror Book Six*
*G is for Genies: A-Z of Horror Book Seven*
*H is for Hell: A-Z of Horror Book Eight*
*I is for Internet: A-Z of Horror Book Nine*
*J is for Jack-o'-Lantern: A-Z of Horror Book Ten*
*K is for Kidnap: A-Z of Horror Book Eleven*
*L is for Lycans: A-Z of Horror Book Twelve*
*M is for Medical: A-Z of Horror Book Thirteen*
*N is for Nautical: A-Z of Horror Book Fourteen*
*O is for Outbreak: A-Z of Horror Book Fifteen*
*It Came from the Darkness: A Charity Anthology*
*Out of the Shadows: A Charity Anthology*
*Hot off the Press: A Charity Anthology*
*Castle Heights: 18 Storeys, 18 Stories*
*Sweet Little Chittering*
*Unceremonious*
*The Nookienomicon*

**Short Story Collections:**

*Embrace the Darkness by P.J. Blakey-Novis*
*Tunnels by P.J. Blakey-Novis*
*The Artist by P.J. Blakey-Novis*
*Karma by P.J. Blakey-Novis*
*The Place Between Worlds by P.J. Blakey-Novis*
*Home by P.J. Blakey-Novis*
*Short Horror Stories by P.J. Blakey-Novis*
*Short Horror Stories Vol.2 by P.J. Blakey-Novis*
*Keep It Inside & Other Weird Tales by Mark Anthony Smith*
*Everything's Annoying by J.C. Michael*
*Six! By Mark Cassell*
*Monsters in the Dark by Donovan 'Monster' Smith*
*Barriers by David F. Gray*
*Love & Other Dead Things by Astrid Addams*
*Bone Carver by Gemma Paul*
*Shadows of Death by Dee Caples*

**Novelettes:**

*The Ivory Tower by Antoinette Corvo*

**Novellas:**

*Four by P.J. Blakey-Novis*
*Dirges in the Dark by Antoinette Corvo*
*The Cat That Caught the Canary by Antoinette Corvo*
*Bow-Legged Buccaneers from Outer Space by David Owain Hughes*
*Spiffing by Tim Mendees*
*A Splintered Soul by Adrian Meredith*
*Scavengers of the Sun by Adrian Meredith*

**Novels:**

*Madman Across the Water by Caroline Angel*
*The Curse Awakens by Caroline Angel*
*Less by Caroline Angel*
*Where Shadows Move by Caroline Angel*
*Origin of Evil by Caroline Angel*
*Origin of Evil: Beginnings by Caroline Angel*
*Exist by Caroline Angel*
*The Vegas Rift by David F. Gray*
*The Broken Doll by P.J. Blakey-Novis*
*The Broken Doll: Shattered Pieces by P.J. Blakey-Novis*
*South by Southwest Wales by David Owain Hughes*
*Any Which Way but South Wales by David Owain Hughes*
*Appletown by Antoinette Corvo*
*Nails by K.J. Sargeant*
*The Eternal by Timothy Friesenhahn*

**Art Books:**

*Demons Never Die by David Paul Harris & P.J. Blakey-Novis*
*Six Days of Violence by P.J Blakey-Novis & David Paul Harris*

**Magazines:**

*Cauldron of Chaos*

## Follow Red Cape Publishing

www.redcapepublishing.com
www.facebook.com/redcapepublishing
www.twitter.com/redcapepublish
www.instagram.com/redcapepublishing
www.pinterest.co.uk/redcapepublishing
www.patreon.com/redcapepublishing
www.ko-fi.com/redcape
www.buymeacoffee.com/redcape